TOWER HAMLETS
D0318596

WITHDRAWN

idea
Library Learning Information
To renew this item call:
0333 370 4700
(Local rate call)
or visit
www.ideastore.co.uk
TOWER HAMLETS
Created and managed by Tower Hamlets Council

THE INVENTORY
IRON FIST

ANDY BRIGGS

SCHOLASTIC

Scholastic Children's Books
An imprint of Scholastic Ltd
Euston House, 24 Eversholt Street, London, NW1 1DB, UK
Registered office: Westfield Road, Southam, Warwickshire, CV47 0RA
SCHOLASTIC and associated logos are trademarks and/or
registered trademarks of Scholastic Inc.

First published in the UK by Scholastic Ltd, 2016

Copyright © Andy Briggs, 2016

The right of Andy Briggs to be identified as
the author of this work has been asserted by him.

ISBN 978 1407 16179 2

A CIP catalogue record for this book
is available from the British Library.

All rights reserved.
This book is sold subject to the condition that it shall not,
by way of trade or otherwise, be lent, hired out or otherwise circulated in
any form of binding or cover other than that in which it is published. No
part of this publication may be reproduced, stored in a retrieval system,
or transmitted in any form or by any means (electronic, mechanical,
photocopying, recording or otherwise) without prior
written permission of Scholastic Limited.

Printed by CPI Group (UK) Ltd, Croydon, CR0 4YY
Papers used by Scholastic Children's Books are made
from wood grown in sustainable forests.

1 3 5 7 9 10 8 6 4 2

This is a work of fiction. Names, characters, places, incidents
and dialogues are products of the author's imagination or are used
fictitiously. Any resemblance to actual people, living or dead,
events or locales is entirely coincidental.

www.scholastic.co.uk

TO DAD, ALWAYS A NEW ADVENTURE...

THE POWER OF FEAR

Pavel Branonov fought for breath as he rushed around the stale-smelling apartment. His trembling hands pulled yellow-paged books off aging shelves; he paused only to scan the first few pages before he moved on to the next.

Time was against him, yet it had to be here...

He suddenly froze, cocking his head to the side as the wail of police sirens grew. They were on to him. He took a deep breath to control the fear welling inside him, then continued searching through the tomes on the shelf.

"Come on, come on," he muttered in Russian. Then

he found it: a small handwritten journal. The yellowing pages were written in spidery cursive. The first page read: IRON FIST IVX – 1987112 – MAJESTIC LEVEL SECURITY PROTOCOLS.

He gasped in surprise – so it was true! For the briefest of moments his mind swirled as endless possibilities stretched before him.

The rhythmic chirping of his mobile phone's timer snapped him back to the moment. He was painfully aware that every beep was a nail in his own coffin.

The sirens were now in the street outside. He had used up all his time. He shoved the book safely into his jacket and stepped over the body blocking the door. He regretted knocking the old man out – he was a colleague Pavel had been fond of – but at least the amnesia stun baton had been painless and he would remember nothing when he awoke.

"Forgive me, comrade," he muttered, and headed out of the squalid apartment and on to the landing.

The wooden floorboards creaked with every step as he dashed for the staircase. Before he could take a step down, a policeman appeared, his pistol waving dangerously in Pavel's direction.

"Halt!"

Pavel did the opposite. He ran back along the corridor to the landing window. The cop's footsteps rattled up the stairs behind him as he strained to prise open the warped wooden frame. With a screech that set his teeth on edge, it juddered open. He clambered through, grazing his knee on the rusting fire escape. He just caught sight of the out-of-breath policeman appearing at the top of the stairs, before rapidly descending the ladder.

Like the rest of the Moscow suburb, the ladder had not been maintained for decades. One too many harsh winters had worn through several rungs, causing the rust to crumble under Pavel's shoe, and he fell to the ground.

He landed hard on his back. At least the recent snow helped cushion his fall, although he felt something crack – maybe a rib. He didn't have time to worry about that. He only had three more minutes to live.

The alleyway into which Pavel had fallen connected to streets in both directions, but he was too disoriented to work out which side of the building he had emerged from. His escape car lay at the front. One or the other direction would have to do.

Pavel stood and immediately slipped on the ice

beneath the snow. He checked his balance. White-hot pain shot though his ankle; it was broken – that explained the cracking noise. Ignoring it, he limped towards the open road ahead. The timer on his phone beeped again, indicating his lifespan had shrunk by a third.

Before he could reach the end of the road, a figure strode into view, blocking his path. For a heart-stopping moment Pavel thought the police had caught up with him.

But it wasn't the police; it was a tall suited figure who was oblivious to the biting temperature. He wore odd yellow-lensed glasses that hid his eyes. His face was impassive, as if some freak accident had robbed him of the ability to move his facial muscles. Pavel only knew him as the Collector. The man's cold ruthlessness had become almost legendary.

The Collector held out his black leather-gloved hand and spoke in flawless Russian, although Pavel doubted that was his native tongue. "Do you have it?"

"The police..." gasped Pavel, pointing over his shoulder.

On cue, the police car skidded into the alleyway. Sirens whooped as the driver struggled to right the fishtailing car as he accelerated towards them.

The Collector raised his hand, extending his fingers. Pavel saw smoke rising from the leather glove. It took a second or two for him to realize that it wasn't smoke, but dense nanoparticles, swarming like bees between the Collector's fingers before shooting towards the police car.

The car struck the dust cloud at speed – and suddenly froze in place. The sirens warbled feebly before falling silent. Pavel couldn't work out what had happened . . . until the vehicle wobbled and began to fall flat.

Flat.

With a complete disregard for conventional physics, the dust had rendered the police car into a *two-dimensional* object. It had width and height but no depth, possessing all the substance of a photograph. Pavel could still see the policemen inside, pounding the windscreen in terror, as if they were trapped in a television screen. The image shattered as it struck the ground, breaking into a billion pixels until the men and car were nothing more than dimensionless molecules in the snow.

Pavel tore his gaze back to the Collector. "How did. . .?"

"Do you have it?" There was a growl of impatience now.

Pavel hesitated. Since entering business with the Collector he had seen things he could never un-see. Terrors that gnawed his conscience and had even driven him to murder. The beep of his phone made the decision for him.

"Yes. It is all in here." He fished the journal from his jacket and handed it to the Collector. "Its last resting place."

Without opening it, the Collector slipped the book into the inside of his jacket. Even with his life on the line, Pavel had to know. "So it's *all* true? The place really exists?"

"Its existence and location was never in question." The Collector tapped the book. "This confirms how Iron Fist *works*. That's the key to my entire operation."

"I have done my part of the deal. Everything you asked. In return you promised me the cure," Pavel said.

The Collector nodded. "I did. And you have it." He did not move.

"What do you mean? Please! Give it to me!" Pavel started to feel the cold seep into his veins, a mixture of the Moscow winter and the sudden sense of betrayal.

"There is no cure. You were never poisoned."

"What? That cannot be..."

"Poison is such a primitive weapon. One I would never stoop to use. The only poison was your own fear. And fear can drive men mad. Make them commit unspeakable acts all in the name of survival." The Collector spoke in a calm, even tone. He wasn't mocking, simply stating a fact.

"You're lying!" Pavel shouted – and then his phone beeped the final alarm, signalling his imminent death. Yet nothing happened. He stared at the Collector with astonishment and contempt. "Y-you made me do those things . . . those terrible things. . ."

"You chose to do them yourself. For fear of your life."

"You manipulated me!"

The Collector laughed as he laid a hand on Pavel's shoulder. It was the first human gesture he had seen from this mysterious man since they had met two weeks ago. "People perform best when they believe they are doing the right thing, comrade. You have been a great asset to the cause. Shadow Helix will know of your accomplishments."

Pavel was suddenly aware that particles were flowing from the fiend's glove and rapidly spreading all over him. He opened his mouth to speak but was unable to utter a sound.

To his horror, he felt himself gently falling backwards, staring skyward – his body possessing nothing more than the thickness of a shadow. . .

DO NOT TOUCH

There's nothing more exhilarating than flying, thought Dev, as he shot at forty miles per hour down the narrow avenue of shelves, seconds before his HoverBoots decided to malfunction and twist him upside down.

His dark hair whipped into his eyes and he gave an involuntary shriek. Rocking his body like a pendulum, Dev attempted to roll himself back upright as a heavy metal shelf rushed to meet him head-on.

It didn't work.

With a grunt, Dev strained to lift his head just enough to prevent it cracking against the shelf.

"WOW!" he exclaimed, then whooped with delight

at surviving the near miss.

That's when the right boot made a loud pop and black smoke spewed from its coolant vents. Now powered by a single heavy boot, Dev was sent spiralling to the floor.

With a terrible scraping noise, the remaining HoverBoot dragged him across the smooth polished floor until he finally thudded into another shelf and the boot died with a death rattle.

Silence flooded the warehouse.

Dev took a deep breath. That joyride hadn't quite gone to plan.

I guess it could have been worse, he thought woozily as he sat up and looked around at the mess.

Dev only became aware of the creaking at the last moment, and looked up in time to see another massive shelf topple like a felled tree. He threw his arms over his head as it crashed down on top of him – and some of the most advanced technology the world was not yet ready for rained down on him.

"Devon?" An apoplectic voice suddenly bellowed from his watch. "Devon Parker? You are in *serious* trouble!"

"Oh, boy," Dev sighed, putting his head in his hands. It *was* worse.

*

The pain was biting as Dev rapidly pulled the plaster off his face. It smarted for a moment, but at least the Heal-o-Plast had repaired the cut made by the falling tech. He gave three short breaths before yanking the second plaster off his arm. It hurt like crazy, but like the one on his face, the deep cut on his forearm had completely healed without leaving even the hint of a scar.

Dev sighed. Like so many items stashed in the Inventory, the Heal-o-Plasts could be used for such good, but instead the authorities had deemed that they were not for public use. Dev could never understand why. Surely instantly healing people was a good thing? He turned to watch his uncle, Charles Parker, straining to the heave the heavy metal shelving units back into their upright position with the help of a grumpy robot called Eema.

"Trust you to be messing about down here," tutted the robot in her best schoolteacher tone.

Eema was a beyond-state-of-the-art artificially intelligent computer system, a marvellous blend of engineering and computer coding, and the Inventory's ruthless security. Eema couldn't simply be copied like a *normal* computer program. She was *special*. Her physical form was a metal sphere two-and-a-half metres in diameter, capable of rolling at up to thirty miles per hour. She could then unfold into segments that formed multiple arms, legs, and even an assortment of weapons. A holographic head, the size of a bowling ball, floated just above her body, like a huge yellow-headed emoji. The usually smiling face looked irritated every time Eema glanced in Dev's direction.

With the shelves back up, Charles Parker and Eema carefully placed the fallen items back in their allocated spaces: a box of Smart-Putty, a digital zodiac detector (which claimed Dev was born under a different star sign every time he used it), a can of anti-graffiti paint and many other banished items. He examined each under a light, looking for the slightest tear, ding or scratch.

The only sounds coming from Dev's uncle were a series of exasperated tuts and sighs. Dev would have rather been told off, shouted at – *anything* but hearing his uncle's trademark disappointed tut. It was psychological warfare and Dev couldn't take much more. The sooner this was over with the better.

Throwing away the scrunched-up Heal-o-Plasts, he decided it was time to help clear up his mess. He bent and picked up a white spherical object.

"NO!" Charles shouted, snatching it from his hands and holding it protectively to his chest, caressing it as if it were a puppy. "Do you have *any* idea what this is?"

Dev shrugged. "Nope." He hated the way his uncle's accusing glare bored into him.

"A Higgs-Bos-Bomb. And do you know what it will do if it's triggered?"

Again that glare, like a loathsome headmaster ready to belittle his student.

Dev decided to play his game. "No, Charles. What will happen?"

Charles Parker's eyes flinched for a second. He hated it when Dev used his proper name. "That's the point. *Nobody* does! That's why you can't just come in here and knock things over like some wild . . . weasel." He shuffled over to the shelf to replace his precious baby.

Dev tried to hide his smile. *Brat* was harsh language coming from his uncle. He picked up a small tube of what looked like mints. He must have dropped them when he crashed. He pocketed them.

"I'm sorry. I didn't mean to do this. I was just checking out those cool-looking HoverBoots. . ." Dev realized playing nice was going to get him out of the warehouse quicker than arguing.

Charles picked up the still-smouldering right boot and looked at it sadly. "The XV-19 HoverBoot prototype from 1936! *Prototype* – that's why it's here in the Inventory; I thought you understood that?"

Dev hung his head. He'd heard it all before and it always annoyed him. Prototypes. Just experiments.

Charles gestured around. "The public is not ready for any of this technology. HoverBoots, rocket packs . . . my gosh, can you imagine what would happen if a bunch of thugs got their hands on the Camo-Jackets?" He carefully placed the sphere back on its special shelf mount. "And you could have been crushed by the shelf," he added as an afterthought.

Dev shook his head; that summed up their relationship perfectly. He was always the afterthought.

"Anyway, I thought you were afraid of heights?" said his uncle.

Dev shrugged. "I wasn't planning on going very high. Just, y'know, fast. I'm not afraid of *fast*." It was crazy. How could he live in a place surrounded by so much potential excitement, so many amazing pieces of kit, yet have one of the most boring lives on the planet?

Charles continued. "The world is in turmoil enough as it is. The Inventory is here to make sure that nothing like *that* gets into the wrong hands to make it worse." He indicated to a large disc-shaped object, about the size of a bus, that was covered in a heavy tarpaulin. Dev guessed it was a recent addition, as it hadn't been there last time he'd been in the section.

"Says who?" The words blurted from Dev's mouth before he could stop them. He edged closer to the massive disc. Curiosity to know exactly what was under the sheet burned deep in his gut. That was his problem – he was curious, like the proverbial cat.

Charles scratched his grey hair, then adjusted his glasses before giving Dev the usual curt answer. "Says the World Consortium."

"Oh, that bunch of unelected suits nobody really knows anything about?"

"That's enough," Charles snapped. There was ice in his voice, and Dev knew instantly that he was on dangerous ground. Charles looked around at the remaining chaos his nephew had wrought and shook his head. "There will be a punishment for this."

"Every day spent with you is a punishment," said Dev out loud, and instantly regretted it. There was no real love between him and his uncle. Theirs was a relationship of convenience. Nevertheless, Charles Parker provided everything for him, and he knew he shouldn't have been so impulsive to speak his thoughts aloud. However, if Charles had heard, he showed no sign of it. Dev heaved a sigh of relief.

Curious and impulsive – two explosive parts of his personality. He wondered which came from his mother and which from his father. He didn't recall ever meeting them, and Charles Parker never spoke about them. Every question was skilfully navigated by his uncle, a verbal ballet that left Dev more muddled than before he'd asked.

Cold light from a half moon hanging low in the sky bathed the small town of Edderton and failed to highlight anything of interest. That was as poetic as Dev could get about his hometown as he looked vacantly across it from the hilltop on which his uncle's farm lay, while beneath it sat the labyrinth of vast interlocking warehouses that made up the Inventory.

Dev's hooded top was pulled tight but did little to warm him. He shivered against the winter nip and thrust his hands deeper into his jacket. He felt bad about the HoverBoot incident, but reminded himself it was only natural to rebel when your life was as unfair as his was. And it wasn't only at home. His mind wandered to the injustice inflicted upon him earlier that day at school. . .

It had been during a hated swimming lesson. (Dev could swim perfectly well, so he didn't see the need for him to prove this to his teacher.) As usual, he had been keeping to himself and ignoring his classmates. Dev had never had a close friend. His classmates had all learned to keep away from the class nerd for fear that he would start to talk about science, some complicated new piece of technology, or a subject that was equally dull.

Dev was well built and he had even overheard girls at school saying he was cute. But the label of nerd had stuck, and his confidence had been dashed. Dev had no choice but to accept his role as the quiet one nobody really paid attention to.

Except for Mason, that is.

If Dev was well built, then Mason was over-built, as if somebody had inflated him at birth but then forgot to turn the air off. He was a blunt instrument. A battering ram with the IQ of a hammer to match. He was popular on account of the raw fact that he would beat up any kid who dared claim he wasn't. It was only Dev who failed to acknowledge Mason's popularity – and occasionally set them on a collision course.

Such as today, when Dev had been preparing to dive into the pool, and Mason had whipped Dev's shorts down – and off – as he hit the water.

Bobbing naked in the middle of the pool as the rest of the class gathered around to laugh and wolf-whistle was not the highlight of Dev's week.

From high on the hilltop, Dev looked at the network of street lights below and wondered which house Mason lived in. There was enough exotic weaponry below his feet to blast the bully's home into orbit.

Or destroy the entire town.

Or worse.

Charles Parker seemed to have forgotten about the punishment that he had threatened. Maybe, thought Dev, he knew that living in Edderton was punishment enough. It was a town so dull, so unaware of the modern world, that the sleepy citizens had no idea that the entire place merely existed just as a cover for the Inventory that lay under his feet.

Only two people could access the Inventory: Charles Parker and Dev.

As long as Dev could remember, he had lived there

with his uncle. The way Charles Parker told the story was that he had been given the job as caretaker two weeks after Dev's mother, Charles's sister, disappeared in mysterious circumstances. She had never been heard from since. Charles claimed he hadn't known what to expect when the World Consortium had asked him to quit his job at some place called the Defence Advanced Research Projects Agency, or DARPA, in America and come here.

Dev often wondered if Charles Parker had been a terrible engineer at DARPA, because surely it was a massive step down to be a caretaker, even if it was to look after one of the most incredible places on earth. (And even if his uncle's strict rules about not playing with anything in the Inventory made living there pointless.)

Dev shouted at the top of his lungs, "As soon as I'm old enough, I'm outta here!"

His voice carried across the empty fields. He was desperate for a new start; a fresh beginning. But for now he was trapped. Friendless, unhappy, and convinced that the rest of the world was having more fun than he was.

DOUBLE TROUBLE

Dev believed that there was life beyond earth. Out in space, maybe in parallel universes. It was unthinkable that mankind was alone in the universe.

He also knew, with absolute certainty, that explaining the concept of school to a higher alien intelligence would be impossible.

It was not that he didn't like school. Well, yes, it *was* that. But only because he knew it *all*. Right from the start, he had found maths straightforward. English was English. History? Well, what use was history to anybody? And he'd been banned from chemistry and home economics for destroying both classrooms with improvised experiments. He had joined the school's karate team, but that was a short-lived when it dawned on him that he was so bad at it that he was effectively volunteering to be beaten up each week.

For a short while, at least, he had loved science. That was, until he'd got past Newton's three laws of motion, blah, blah, blah, and wanted to know about more advanced concepts, such as quantum string theory and gravitational waves. It was at that point that his teacher had pulled a face and gently coaxed the class back to more mundane things such as magnetism.

Dev suspected that his teacher didn't actually know the answer to his questions.

The day ground on, and already people seemed to have forgotten about the previous day's swimming pool incident. Dev almost wished they hadn't. Was he so forgettable that even the most embarrassing moment of his life didn't register interest in these people? How mixed up was his life that he was angry that *nobody* was taunting him?

With these confused emotions battling in his thoughts, he sat down at his desk and was surprised to find an invite to a party after school.

To Lot's birthday party, to be precise.

Tonight.

Lot was one of the few people in school, in the entire town, whom Dev would call "interesting". She was top of the school karate team, always the first with her hand in the air in class. Outside school she was a one-girl road hazard, riding her bike around town as if the apocalypse was pursuing her. Despite her infectious smile, she intimidated Dev.

And why would she invite him to her birthday party? They had never spoken.

For the rest of the day, Dev debated if he should go. He even pondered if he should ask her whether the invite was an accident. Instead he did what he usually did and kept his head down, avoided people and read in the corner of the library while everybody else frittered their time away playing football on the internet or forming gangs just to avoid him.

Dev glanced at his watch and chuckled to himself. The piece of technology on his wrist was a hundred times more advanced than any phone, yet he couldn't show anybody. If he did, would people still consider him uninteresting?

With a deflated sigh he guessed they probably would.

*

Clouds mugged the sun as the end of the day approached, threatening rain.

Reluctant to go straight home, Dev decided to cycle to the address printed on the invite. It wasn't as if his uncle would miss him. Dev knew he had a degree of freedom that most kids his age would be envious of. His uncle never demanded that he come home at a certain time, didn't give him many chores to do (aside from sweeping the nonexistent dust in the Inventory and washing his own clothes), and with no other relatives, there were no family get-togethers. But while all this would excite most of his classmates, it simply added to Dev's feeling of being out of place.

Lot's house was large and stood on the edge of the town, not quite as far out as his home on the farm.

Dev could hear music belting from the back garden, but he pulled the crumpled invite from his pocket to double-check the address anyway. He felt something small and round beside it, and made a mental note that he still had the mints – they would probably have to do as his dinner. If he stayed long at the party then he wouldn't be back in time for whatever his uncle had cooked – which would be a good thing. Charles Parker considered "fresh" to be something that had just oozed out of the microwave.

Taking a deep breath, Dev laid his bike against a tree in the front yard and walked around the back of the house.

It was definitely the right place. A DJ was playing on a small stage and lasers strobed through the smoke billowing from a machine. An inflatable obstacle course was crawling with teams of kids armed with laser tag guns, and the centrepiece was a shallow plastic pool that was filled with foam and kids chucking frothy balls at one another. Flaming heat lamps kept the winter's chill at bay and lent a tropical atmosphere to the party.

It was, in a word, *awesome*.

Dev walked through it with a growing sense of anticipation. Lot was a popular girl. He recognized many people, but had only talked to few of them. He took a cold chicken wing from the buffet and wandered around, trying to spot the birthday girl.

It took him a few minutes to find Lot among the scrum of people, seated in a gaming chair playing the latest first-person shooter. The entire game was projected on a large screen. Dev was impressed.

He saw her glance over and waved. That prompted a confused look from Lot, who quickly turned back to the screen as the boy next to her seized the advantage and shot her character. Lot threw down her controller and a heated argument ensued.

Sensing he was the cause of her defeat, Dev took a tactical step backwards – straight into the hulking figure of Mason.

"Sorry," mumbled Dev, trying to step aside.

Mason moved quickly, blocking his path and forcing Dev to walk into him again. "What was that?" cried Mason. He looked at his two cronies on either side. "You see that? He's trying to cause trouble."

Dev sensed danger. More than that, he sensed a trap. Mason had conveniently positioned him next to the foam pool. Dev felt his stomach lurch – he wasn't going to fall for the same trick twice.

"Stop trying to pick a fight with me!" said Mason in the phoniest voice Dev had ever heard. He glanced around and saw all eyes were on them. Surely somebody would intervene and put a stop to it?

Mason moved with a sudden swiftness. Dev felt a firm hand shove him in the chest while another tried to grab his belt to yank his trousers down. Dev wasn't going to let that happen this time. With both hands he kept his trousers from falling – but that left him off balance. He flew backwards – landing hard in the shallow water, splashing foam everywhere.

Even in a few centimetres of water, Dev was soaked. He quickly stood, wiping the foam from his eyes. As he did so he became aware that everybody was laughing. For several eternally long seconds he realized that Mason had succeeded in his mission – Dev's trousers were now around his ankles.

It was even more embarrassing than the swimming pool.

Lot was shoving her way through the crowd and looked at the scene with a mixture of disapproval and annoyance. Dev's cheeks burned with embarrassment. He pulled his trousers up – the contents of his pocket spilling into the pool. His fists clenched of their own accord and, as he stared at Mason's big grinning face, he felt rage surge though him.

With an athletic bound he was surprised he was capable of, Dev launched himself at Mason. At that exact same moment, the foam around him exploded in a fury of bubbles and another shape emerged. It was the same size and shape as Dev, although its features were translucent – almost watery. It converged on Mason at the same time Dev did – two fists punching the bully's startled face.

Dev landed with a crouch – and so did the watery figure. Mason was lifted off his feet and sent sprawling into a buffet table. Food scattered in every direction, forcing the crowd to run from flying nuggets and jelly.

Dev caught his breath as he looked around. The figure had vanished. Perhaps it had been a figment of his stressed imagination? But then he saw astonished faces watching him. Lot's mouth hung open as she stared.

An angry adult hauled Dev to his feet. There was shouting, but Dev wasn't really listening. He was surprised by his actions: proud, even. He'd never thought he possessed the courage to strike back, but Mason had succeeded in pushing him over a line.

For the first time, he had stood up for himself and it felt wonderful. Dev wondered what else he was really capable of if he put his mind to it.

PREPARATION

The Collector inhaled the cool, briny air as the breeze picked up. He'd always felt more at home along the coast, away from the polluted cities. If all went smoothly, polluted cities would be a thing of the past and the planet would thank him. Eventually.

"Everything is checked, sir," said Lee as the digital scanner embedded in his black-rimmed glasses read the digital manifest for the crates being unloaded from the tramp steamer.

The aging boat looked as though it wouldn't make the return voyage to its home port of Sierra Leone, but that was just a ruse. Underneath the rusted hull was a state-of-the-art carbon-fibre body with an engine powerful enough to outrun the most curious customs officer. It was part of Shadow Helix's own private fleet of military-class vehicles that could take them anywhere in the world.

The Collector watched as his team moved back and forth along the quay, loading the crates on to the waiting army trucks. He didn't expected anything to be amiss – his suppliers knew the dreadful penalty for failure – but it was better to be sure. The Collector never left anything to chance. Every move had been carefully rehearsed.

The thump of something heavy snapped his attention back to the quay. Kwolek had dropped a crate. Everybody around her had frozen in horror, as if expecting it to explode.

"Sorry," she said, swiping at the long strand of red hair that flapped across her eyes.

The muscled man next to her began shouting in Italian, then switched to English. "You stupid ox! Be more careful!"

Lee looked up from the manifest and winced. Calling Kwolek an ox could turn out worse than dropping a dozen crates.

Kwolek moved with her usual deliberateness. She picked the crate up with both hands – a task that had required two burly longshoremen just moments ago – and placed it on to the truck. The contents were so heavy that the suspension groaned and the body of the truck lowered a few centimetres.

"See," she said, scowling, "I didn't blow us all sky high." She turned to the Italian and grabbed the scruff of his neck, lifting him off the floor without the slightest effort due to the bionic implants that had replaced most of her muscles. "And call me an ox again and I will collapse that fat head of yours." She dropped him and clapped her hands in front of his nose. The noise sounded like a thunderclap and made the big man jump. "Like so!"

Lee approached the Collector as the team continued loading the trucks.

"I did warn you about her temper," he said. The Collector didn't answer, so Lee continued. "Everything is on schedule. We'll be ready to leave within the hour."

"You have the access schematics?"

Lee tapped the side of his glasses. Only he could see the head-up display projected on the inside of the lens that told him the state of his latest cyberattack. Lee had once been part of the world's most notorious hacking group, known only as Anonymous, but he had since left the secretive movement to work for the Collector. As for the identity of the mysterious Shadow Helix that the Collector worked for, that was beyond Lee's skills to uncover.

"Working on that as we speak. Just manage your expectations; that security is so tight and advanced, we won't really know what we're up against until we're in there."

The Collector's voice turned ice cold. "We are depending on you, Lee. There will be no help from within."

"Relax." Lee forced a laugh. "We'll hack them as we go along. But there is nothing I can do for the last step. Iron Fist is beyond even me."

The Collector turned his gaze back to the quay.

"But not me."

THE FARM

The following day at school Dev imagined he was a special forces soldier avoiding the enemy, who, in this case, was everybody who had been present at the party.

Slinking into the background was a gift he had long used to avoid trouble. However, word spread like wildfire about the incident. It ranged from pure hysteria that Mason had pulled Dev's trousers down in the middle of the party, to the spectacle of Dev punching Mason to the ground – through to rumours that the bully was planning painful revenge.

You just can't win, thought Dev despondently.

He tried to work out just what had happened during

the brief incident. The odd figure that had appeared next to him hadn't been a figment of his imagination after all. Some pupils claimed to have seen it too, and whispers circled that Dev knew some arcane magic tricks.

Typical idiots, thought Dev as he cycled home, grateful that a weekend lay between him and more school. He knew everything, no matter how bizarre, could be explained by science. Even magic.

There was only one way to explain the strange figure. It must have been caused by something he had inadvertently picked up in the Inventory – and that could only have been those small discs that he had thought were mints. They were now missing from his pocket. They *must* have been responsible for his doppelgänger.

What bothered Dev more was the fact it was out of character for his uncle to overlook a missing item, no matter how small. What could have been distracting him? Was Dev really such a terrible hindrance?

As he left the town and powered down the lane leading to the farm, Dev was so lost in his thoughts that he didn't see the figure on a bike up ahead until it turned to block his path.

Dev squeezed his brakes and skidded to a halt,

sending a curtain of mud shooting into the air. His first thought was that Mason had finally caught up with him – but a second glance was more surprising.

It was Lot.

"I've been looking for you all day," she said, eyeing him with suspicion.

Dev couldn't meet her eyes. "Look . . . I'm really sorry for what happened last night."

"You mean making a colossally embarrassing scene at my party?" She folded her arms.

Dev was suddenly angry. Why should he be apologizing? It wasn't his fault. "No. Not for that. For turning up! I shouldn't have been so stupid to believe you would have actually invited me in the first place."

He nudged his bike past her and continued cycling. How dare she make him feel so bad? He was surprised when he heard her voice next to him a few seconds later as she caught up.

"I didn't *not* invite you," she said, her tone softer. "I just didn't see the point."

"Oh, thanks. That's so much better."

She gave a theatrically loud sigh. "Because you never come to *anything.* When I joined in primary school I invited you to every single one of my parties but you never came." That surprised Dev. He didn't recall ever being invited to *anything*. "And you don't exactly go out of your way to talk to me in school." She let the words hang in the air.

Of course. Dev suddenly worked it out. "Mason faked the invite," he said "The fact he spelt everything correctly threw me."

Lot snorted with laughter. "He just wanted to embarrass you in public again," she said. "But I think you won this time. That was a nice trick you pulled."

They rode on in silence. Out of the corner of his eye, Dev noticed that she was studying him.

"My grandpa used to do magic on stage so I know how a lot of the tricks are done," added Lot. "But that was quite something."

Dev felt his cheeks burn. All his life he had been sworn to secrecy about the existence of the Inventory. It was something that had been drummed into him before he had even been able to spell his name, and this was the first time he had ever come remotely close to somebody asking suspicious questions.

"Yeah ... well ... I can be surprising like that." It was a lame reply, but he didn't trust himself not to reveal anything incriminating.

After several minutes of idle chit-chat they reached the gates of the farm. Lot took in the small cottage and the couple of barns visible from the road. A few sheep milled around in a pen and bleated when they saw her.

"Nice place," she said approvingly. "Do you have many animals?"

Dev opened the gate just enough to roll his bike through and closed it before Lot had a chance to follow him.

"Oh, a few," he said. "Well, it was great talking to you. I'm glad you're not too angry about . . . y'know."

"You could always invite me in." Lot beamed her infectious smile, highlighting the freckles on her cheeks. For a fleeting instant, Dev thought she would look at home as a rock singer, always on tour, always having fun . . . he tore his mind away from that.

"My uncle doesn't like surprise visitors . . . maybe another time."

Her smile dropped. She stared at him for a long moment and even managed to look hurt. "Oh, OK. No problem." She turned her bike around and began cycling away. "See you tomorrow."

Dev waved. "See you tomorrow."

It wasn't until he had stowed his bike in the barn that he realized tomorrow was Saturday.

THE APPROACH

The convoy of four trucks trundled through the night. Powerful headlights illuminated the dark road ahead and nothing more. It was as if they were driving into an abyss. Windscreen wipers whacked back and forth, batting away the deluge that fell from the heavens.

In the cab of the lead truck, Lee was sandwiched in between a huge driver and one of the thuggish mercenaries whose name he had already forgotten. The truck rocked from side to side along the bumpy minor roads that they were taking so as not to draw attention to themselves. Lee had a computer tablet on his knee and was swiping through pages of technical information while the thug read a comic, laughing loudly at regular intervals. Every time he laughed his body would shake, squashing Lee further.

"Do you mind?" said Lee impatiently. They had been driving for four hours and already he wanted to throw the mercenary from the moving vehicle. "I need to concentrate."

The big man glanced at the tablet screen and grunted dismissively. "You waste your time with all of this old stuff."

Lee sighed. "Old stuff? This is the history of Iron Fist. You have read up, right? You know its importance?" He tapped the screen. "Iron Fist was a top-secret project, the ultimate defence system. That's what it was designed for. But at the core is this— " He held up the screen but the mercenary wasn't listening; his attention was back on his comic. Lee shook his head in despair. "Idiot," he muttered under his breath. He turned back to the tablet – before becoming aware that the big man had heard him and was glaring in his direction.

"What kind of name is Lee, anyway?" the mercenary asked suddenly.

"A code name. Like yours . . . whatever it is. I forget."

"It is Volta. He invented . . . *stuff.*"

Lee sighed. "The light bulb, for example."

"*Si*. Yes. Useful things. And *Lee*?"

Lee smirked and shook his head. "I'll let you figure that out," he muttered. He was thankful that the operation was about to begin.

SNOOPING AROUND

The veins on Charles Parker's temples pulsed so hard, Dev could only stare and wait to see if his uncle's head would explode.

"It was completely unscheduled." Despite the anger on his face, Charles's voice was low and even.

"It was only a party. And not a very good one at that."

Dev glanced around the kitchen to see if there was an obvious reason his uncle was behaving so oddly. As usual, there was no lovingly cooked meal lying cold on the table or surprise pizza delivery – deliveries to the house were forbidden on pain of constant moaning. There was no apparent reason for the outburst.

Charles opened his mouth, but stopped whatever it was he was about to say. After an awkward pause, he simply muttered, "You can't just wander off." He pointed to Dev's watch. "And I think that needs repairing."

"Can I go now? I have homework to do."

Charles nodded and dismissed him with a wave of the hand. Dev quickly left the room. That brief exchange had told him all he needed to know. Dev had disabled the tracking abilities he had discovered buried in his watch so that he could wander around the Inventory without raising suspicion. But it was now apparent that he was under constant surveillance no matter where he was. The prison might have no walls, but Dev couldn't shake the feeling that he was a prisoner in his own life.

"Yellow Zone. Authorization verified," purred Eema's smooth female voice.

Dev removed his hand from the scanner and the massive titanium door in front of him rolled open with the faintest of pneumatic hisses. The lights in the hangar flicked to life in a wave, revealing numerous aisles of metal racks that stretched from floor to ceiling.

Dev smiled. "Thank you, Eema." Despite her calm tones, he knew she was still angry with him for bypassing the security systems so he could play with the HoverBoots.

He just wasn't sure if Eema was angry that he had corrupted the security, or that a kid had outsmarted the supercomputer.

With a sigh, Dev stepped through the portal. A vacuum cleaner was strapped to his back. He switched the tiny motor on and made a pretence of sucking up a few atoms of dust. There was no dust, of course. Each zone was hermetically sealed, with the air pumped in through a series of advanced filters to ensure no chemical poisons could infiltrate the Inventory. The entire storage facility had been designed not just to withstand a nuclear attack, but a direct meteor impact. The idea that a few motes of dust could be an issue was laughable.

One of Charles Parker's few rules was that his nephew carry out a few housekeeping chores at the weekend, despite the fact the entire facility was automated and there were gadgets on the shelves that were so advanced, they could make housework a thing of the past. Charles Parker claimed it bred character, but all Dev thought it did was encourage boredom.

Today, however, it allowed him to do a little investigation.

Dev walked down the towering aisles, reaching the occasional junction that stretched away in a perfectly straight line or ended in another door leading to a further secure section. He knew the layout off by heart so didn't rely on the coloured lines that ran along each aisle. Occasionally they would run in parallel, like a subway train map, before branching off to their own designated section. He was in the Yellow Zone right now. He suspected that there had once been a logical colour-coordinated method of storing the gadgets and gizmos, but his uncle has long since abandoned any obvious way of cataloguing them, as the rate of invention had been too much to keep up with.

Only the Red Zone was special. This housed what his uncle termed "discoveries" rather than inventions. Dev wasn't entirely sure what that meant, other than that it was one of several zones he was never allowed access to.

Without thinking, Dev navigated to the shelf he had nearly cracked his head open on while riding the HoverBoots. Charles Parker had placed everything back with obsessive precision. Some items, such as the Higgs-

Bos-Bomb, now lay behind a shimmering energy shield, to ensure curious hands couldn't touch them again. Others sat behind plain mesh cages, while further items were loose on the shelves.

Dev quickly found one such item, packaged in a pale blue cardboard box that had faded over the years. The illustration showed a grinning kid reaching out, a shimmering apparition next to him mimicking his movement. The text PRISM-BUDDY was printed across it. From the design, Dev guessed it must have been made in the 1950s.

He shook the box, spilling several small discs. They looked just like mints, exactly what he had in his pocket during Lot's party. He turned the box over to read the instructions:

> DROP INTO WATER TO CREATE YOUR OWN PRISM-BUDDY – AN EXACT WATERY REPLICA OF YOU. *H2O-H WHAT FUN!*

Dev held up his watch to a small QR code on the shelf. It connected wirelessly to the Inventory's archive, and the relevant holographic documents floated over his watch's screen. Not everything was properly catalogued in the Inventory. There were many items his uncle had puzzled over the use of for years – but not the Prism-Buddy, clearly. The small ads section of an old comic book immediately appeared on his screen, showing the Prism-Buddy along with magic kits, camouflage gear and anything else a growing kid might want to spend their cash on. Charles Parker had explained that a lot of revolutionary gadgets were sold in the backs of comic books before the authorities had a chance to clamp down and prohibit the items.

It had taken Dev a while to understand that a pair of X-ray specs was not just harmless fun. In the wrong hands they could be used to see into bank vaults, discover military or state secrets and turn the clumsiest person into an astute thief. The most innocent gadget could be used for terrible purposes in the wrong hands.

The Inventory had been created to ban such items and store them away until the world was ready to use them – which Dev assumed would be *never.*

He carefully placed the Prism-Buddy box back on the shelf and resumed pretending to clean. His thoughts drifted back to what Lot had told him about not responding to invites. What had she meant? Had his uncle hidden them from him? Why would he do that?

He was so lost in thought that he jumped in shock as a whooping alarm suddenly echoed through the hangar. It wasn't the two-tone fire alarm though; it was something he had never heard before.

Dev's watch vibrated, the screen indicating a call from his uncle. He tapped the screen to answer and a small hologram of his uncle's head appeared.

"What's the matter?"

Charles Parker's voice sounded strained. "Devon, come up to the house immediately. We have a problem. Somebody has tripped the intruder alarm."

AN UNWELCOME VISITOR

Doors thundered closed behind Dev as he raced back through the aisles and out of the hangar. For years he had begged his uncle to activate the Vacuum-Pods that ran around the complex. These small spherical pods were designed to take people rapidly over huge distances to the furthest reaches of the building. Tunnels up to two miles long separated some of the hangars. Charles Parker had refused, saying they were a security hazard – although Dev suspected it was really to stop him snooping around. On a good day, his uncle had allowed him a Segway, but that had been confiscated when he'd used it to reach a far-flung storage unit and sneak an invisibility gun outside, where he'd zapped a few sheep. It had taken days to find them all.

Dev was out of breath when he reached the express elevator. In this one, the compartment was small, but some of the Inventory's freight elevators were so big a lorry could be parked inside. On the other side of the complex, a hangar roof opened up to the size of a football stadium to allow even larger objects to be lowered in. Dev had watched in awe the time an advanced aircraft carrier had been lowered down and taken to a dry dock deep within the Blue Zone.

Several years ago, Dev had watched a fleet of World Consortium military helicopters lowering something else into the distant hangar. He had never discovered what it was exactly, but it was one of the few times that teams of research scientists had flocked to the Inventory. They had stayed on the farm for several weeks and for once Dev could recall a family atmosphere in his home. Some of the scientists had even played baseball with him. But they, like everybody else in his life, had upped and left one day without any warning.

The express elevator shot up the ten floors to ground level. The doors opened to a windowless room filled with screens mounted around a central command console. This command bunker was located in a barn opposite the farmhouse. Surveillance cameras combed every angle of the property above, and the Inventory's corridors below. An array of sensors monitored every approach – they could even sense the heartbeat of the occasional jogger who ran down the country lane beside the house.

Charles Parker spun around in the control seat and glared disapprovingly. He stabbed a finger at the screen. "What is *that*?"

Dev followed the finger and replied on autopilot. "That is a girl."

He did a double-take at the screen.

That was Lot, sitting on the farm gate.

"The female is identified as Devon's girlfriend," said Eema, almost smugly.

"She is not!" said Dev in a voice that was a little too high-pitched. He lowered it. "She is not my girlfriend."

"She is a girl. She is your friend," said Eema. "It doesn't take Fermat's last theorem to work out that puzzle."

"What is she doing here?" Charles Parker asked, his gaze flicking back to the screen. "You know the rules. No visitors."

Dev knew the rules all right. He'd argued that even prisoners had visitors, but his uncle had been unwavering. No visitors. No parties . . . *and no friends.*

"I didn't invite her."

"You brought her here yesterday," Eema chimed in with increasing smugness.

"She followed me!"

"Shall I prime the laser defence system?" asked Eema.

"No!" shouted Dev. He was angry that both his uncle and an overgrown computer were blaming him for Lot's appearance. And he was angry at Lot for just turning up. Well, a little bit angry but mostly curious.

"I'll go and talk to her," he said hastily as he saw her clamber over the gate.

Dev hurried from the barn and sprinted around the back of the farmhouse before Lot had a chance to reach the front door.

"Lot?" he said, trying to sound surprised.

She grinned at him. "Morning."

He drew level with her, subtly positioning himself so that her attention was drawn away from the house and back towards the front gate.

"I didn't expect to see you here."

Lot looked surprised. "Really? I did say I'd see you tomorrow."

"Ah, I assumed you'd gotten confused and thought it was a school day."

Lot shook her head and began walking over to a barn. "Nah. I don't get confused that easily."

Dev quickly blocked her path. "You can't go in there."

"Why not?"

"It's dangerous. The whole farm is . . . dangerous," he said lamely.

"Dangerous? What's in there?" She smirked and slipped past him before he could do anything to stop her.

Several sheep peered out of the barn from behind a gate. They bleated at her, then continued eating from a trough.

"Ooh, dangerous," teased Lot. "I've never been on a farm before," she added. "Can you believe that?"

"Look, my uncle really doesn't like people—" Dev began, but Lot wasn't listening. Her attention was back on the sheep.

"My dad's a pilot for the air force. He let me go up with him a few times in his jet. That's more what I'd call dangerous."

"Wait, your dad took you up in a jet?" Dev couldn't mask his jealousy. Lot nodded. "That sounds amazing."

Lot was already walking towards the next barn. "First few times it is. But then you get used to it. Like I bet you're used to the farm. What's in this one? Killer chickens?"

Dev blocked her path. "There's nothing in there. Please, my uncle isn't the most fun person in the world. He'll go bonkers." He could imagine Charles Parker shouting angrily at the security screens. Secrecy was more important than fun or family, his uncle had made that abundantly clear. Dev had seen the effects of the array of memory-wiping devices stored under their feet, which his uncle had not hesitated to use on trespassers.

"I thought we could hang out."

"Why would you want to do that?"

"I felt bad for what happened at my party."

"That wasn't your fault."

"And I thought you could show me how you did that magic trick." Lot smiled at Dev's confused expression; it was a smile that said *gotcha*. "You know, the impossible one you did at my party."

Dev mentally kicked himself for being slow on the uptake. "Sorry. A magician never reveals his tricks."

Lot shrugged, then abruptly stepped around him and ran into the barn.

Dev darted after her. "Hey! I said you couldn't go in there!"

But he was too late; she was already inside. Shafts of sunlight speared through the barn's broken roof slats, seeming to form a cage of light around the car-sized object covered by a tarpaulin. It was one of the latest additions to the Inventory. Dev and his uncle were going to categorize it later that afternoon. Teasing glimpses of dangling pipework hung below the reach of the canvas. An old crate had been upended and an open toolbox lay on top. It looked just like a car was being repaired – although Dev knew what lay under the sheet was anything but.

Lot slowly reached out her hand to pull the sheet back.

Dev gripped her wrist and sharply pulled her hand away. "Really, you can't touch that."

She shot him a puzzled look – but before she could protest, a clatter of collapsing wood made them both spin around.

Dev's reactions kicked in and he pulled Lot aside as an old wooden hayloft above them crashed down, whipping up a cloud of mouldy straw. A heavy wooden spar slammed down next to Lot – a centimetre closer and it would have cracked her head open.

A figure rolled out of the hay, coughing and choking. Dev snatched a wrench from the toolbox and raised it threateningly as the figure stood, swaying slightly.

"Mason?" exclaimed Dev in astonishment. Dressed in a khaki jacket and black jeans, Mason was doubled over, spitting dust and straw from his mouth. He held up one hand to fend off the wrench. "You're trespassing, which means I have every right to whack your brains out."

"Don't," wheezed Mason. He was fumbling for something in his pocket.

Dev tensed. He was expecting the thug to draw a weapon. His imagination screamed that it would be a knife – or a gun. He wouldn't put anything past Mason.

Lot placed a hand on Dev's and gently forced him to lower the wrench. It was then that Dev saw that the bully was clutching an asthma inhaler. He took two deep slugs from it. His eyes were bloodshot, streaming with tears.

"Hay fever," he wheezed.

Dev stared at Mason, who was fighting for breath, and wondered how he could ever have seen him as a threat. However, this was no time to be sympathetic.

"You're trespassing," Dev repeated. "I'm calling the cops."

Mason held up his hand. "No. I didn't mean. . . I just wanted to know where you lived. So I followed her." He nodded towards Lot.

Lot noticed the suspicious look Dev was giving her. "Don't look at me like that. I didn't know he was *stalking* me."

"Following," Mason corrected. Warily he regarded the wrench in Dev's hand. "Nobody at school knew where you lived."

"I like to keep it that way. Which still doesn't explain why you're here. Were you planning to try and get your own back?"

Mason didn't answer, but the flicker of a smile betrayed the truth. That had been exactly his plan. Dev felt his stomach knot. Couldn't he even feel safe in his own home?

He raised the wrench again. "Well, beat it or I beat you – or shove hay in your face." Mason's eyes narrowed and Dev knew he had touched on a sore point. "And if my uncle finds you were here then it will get a whole lot worse. Out."

He marshalled Lot and Mason from the barn,

ensuring Mason kept several paces ahead. They made straight for the gate. Dev could feel the unseen security system monitoring their every step. Even though he was getting rid of the trespassers, he knew there would be hell to pay once he had explained things to his uncle.

"You're not throwing me out too, are you?" protested Lot.

"You brought him here, *Lottie.*" Dev knew the use of her full name – as when people called him Devon – was an act of war. He had expected her to protest, but she didn't, and her silence infuriated him further. He felt stupid for believing she had come just to spend time with him.

Dev was so lost in his thoughts that it took several moments for him to realize that Lot and Mason had stopped in their tracks. They were looking at a convoy of army trucks heading down the lane towards the farm. Oh dear, this could be bad. Dev racked his brain. Had his uncle mentioned anything about a delivery today? With Lot and Mason here, that would be awful timing.

At that moment a huge explosion erupted behind the farm and, for the second time that day, the intruder alarm screamed urgently.

THEY'RE HERE...

"We are under attack! Devon, get to the bunker *now*!"

Dev was running even before his wristwatch chimed with Charles Parker's frantic instructions. The bunker was three hundred metres ahead and Dev felt his heart pound and his legs turn to jelly as he ran, dragging Lot and Mason alongside him. He flinched as a drab green military helicopter buzzed low overhead and he caught a glimpse of smoke rising from the rocket launcher strapped to its side. A bright flame of light, and another missile shot out.

"DOWN!" yelled Dev, tackling Lot to the floor.

They landed hard, seconds before the barn exploded

and a wall of heat washed over them as an orange fireball punched through the air.

Dev could hear the bleats of incinerating sheep, punctuated by Mason's shrill scream as a smouldering sheep's head landed next to him.

Lot slapped Mason hard across the cheek. "Pull yourself together!" She raised the severed sheep's head. The animal was still chewing, sparks flying from its neck, a tangle of wires and servomotors dangling loose. "A . . . a robot?" she gasped.

Dev looked back at the gate as the lead truck smashed through it at speed. The gate collapsed, enormous wheels crushing Lot's bike.

By the time the vehicle skidded to a halt, Dev was on his feet and running around the farmhouse. Ahead, the reinforced doors to the bunker outhouse were already spiralling closed. Inside he could see his uncle's back, hunched over a bank of screens and controls.

Dev forced himself to run faster, shoving Lot and Mason ahead of him. He leapt through the rapidly closing portal as it sealed with a deep boom of finality that shook the bunker.

Dev was panting hard as he studied the bank of monitors on the wall of the bunker. The four trucks had spread out around the farmhouse, troops jumping from the back. The helicopter whirled overhead, obscured by the thick black smoke cloud from the barn.

When he could finally catch his breath, Dev asked his uncle, "Who are they?"

Charles Parker was staring past Dev's shoulder. "That's exactly what I was asking myself." His tone indicated he wasn't talking about the attacking helicopter.

Dev followed his uncle's gaze and turned to see Lot and Mason standing at the door, looking around the bunker with wide eyes. He knew they shouldn't be here.

"What was I supposed to do? I couldn't leave them out there." He scowled at Mason. "Well, one of them I could have. . ." he added under his breath.

The bunker gently shook. Then the doors opened once again.

"Out," barked Charles Parker

"You've got to be kidding," said Mason, unable to disguise the panic in his voice. "There are crazy terrorists out there!"

"Out!" Charles Parker jabbed a finger towards the door they had entered through.

Lot and Mason turned, and were surprised to see

that beyond the door wasn't a farm but a smooth-floored tunnel lit by strips of bright lights.

"What is this place?" asked Lot in awe.

With a rapid but imperceptible motion, the bunker had descended into the Inventory below. It was standard procedure during an attack. Dev stepped out into the corridor. They were at a T-junction, one passageway stretched ahead, while further corridors curved out of sight either side. Lot and Mason slowly followed him.

"We're ten storeys underground. They can't get here." Dev regarded his new companions' confused looks and held out his arms like a showman. "Welcome to the Inventory." His smile evaporated like moisture in a furnace when he spotted his uncle's frosty expression.

"Lockdown complete," said Eema from across the public address system.

There was a heavy rolling noise behind them, and Dev's hand covered his eyes in despair as Eema's armoured husk rounded the corner and bore down on them.

"And that is. . .?" asked Mason in a trembling voice.

"And that is the *security*," sighed Dev.

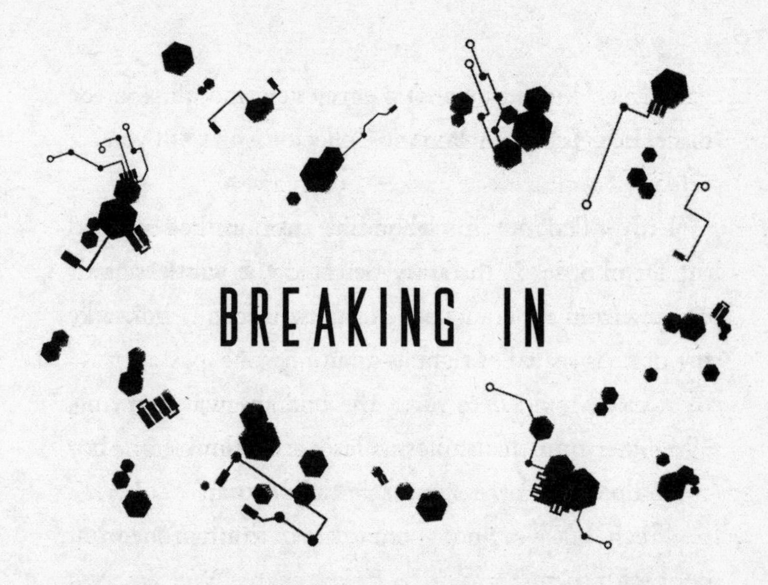

BREAKING IN

Lee stepped out of the lead truck as it pulled up beside the farmhouse. He secured a respirator over his nose and mouth to filter out the cloying black smoke. The skies chose that moment to start snowing, the pure white flakes at odds with the scorched earth.

He strode down the line of the trucks as the team struggled to unload the crates. Even Volta wheezed as he lifted a box. Only Kwolek was making it look easy, single-handedly lifting the heaviest of the crates.

Lee joined her, pulling his suit jacket tighter against the chill. He looked around the farm with a doubtful frown. "Sure hope this is the right place."

Kwolek kicked a robotic sheep's head. "This is the place, Lee. Try and relax, the Collector won't kill you . . . yet."

Lee pulled out his phone as they walked around the farmhouse. It instantly detected the subtle signals coming from the complex beneath their feet. "Looks like the place is sealed as tight as a nut."

Kwolek nodded towards the box she was carrying. "We have sonic drills, plasma laser and atomizers. They could open up Fort Knox like a can of tuna!"

"Yeah, but we're not going to get in through the front door with them."

They stopped around the back of the house. Where the bunker used to stand, a small patch of bubbling dirt was changing from red to black as the molten ground cooled. Lee pulled his suit sleeve away from his watch. A small hologram of the Collector appeared.

"We are here. The bunker was kitted with a plasma cutter. No need for a lift shaft; it just melted through the earth like a knife through butter, sealing the rock back together overhead so we can't follow it."

The Collector nodded. "There are other ways in. See to it."

"Yes, sir."

Kwolek suddenly spoke up before the hologram faded. "There were only supposed to be two of them down there, the man and the boy. Who were the other two kids?"

The image of the Collector turned to stare at her. Even though it was merely a hologram, Kwolek felt a chill run through her. Very few people had ever filled Kwolek with fear, but her new boss went straight to the top of that list.

After what felt like minutes, the Collector finally spoke. "They are of no concern."

Kwolek felt a sense of relief when his image disappeared. She would rather face the lethal defences of the Inventory below than speak to the Collector again any time soon.

LOCKDOWN

Mason and Lot recoiled as the sphere bore down on them at speed. Only Dev held his ground, knowing that Eema would stop in time. With perfect precision the husk stopped inches from him. Panels etched along her surface sprang open with the faintest hum from the electromagnetic motors – and the machine fluidly unfolded, the central body now balanced on two huge circular segmented wheels, like a roller skater. Eema's emoji head appeared, the giant yellow face glowering at them.

"Hey, Eema," sighed Dev.

Eema studied Mason and Lot. Mason took a nervous

step backwards, but Lot couldn't keep the smile from her face. She reached out and ran her fingers across the machine. "Wow. . ."

A pair of arms suddenly extended from Eema's husk, armed with lethal-looking cannons, the end of the barrels glowing with ominous intent. Lot snatched her hand away.

"The Inventory is now in lockdown. Two intruders detected," barked Eema as she stabbed the weapons closer to Mason and Lot.

Dev stepped in front of her, waving his arms. "No, no, no! They're with me!"

Dev spun round to see that his uncle had appeared. Stepping into the corridor from the bunker, he waved Eema away. The machine retreated, but didn't lower its weapons.

"They're *guests,* Eema." Charles spat the unfamiliar word out. "Take them and Devon to the canteen."

"Canteen?" said Dev. "We're not hungry. And in case it escaped your attention, we are under attack!"

Charles Parker circled Lot and Devon, regarding them with mistrust. "And in case it escaped *your* attention, you violated every security protocol when you brought these two down here . . . at the very same instant we were attacked." He lapsed into silence for a moment, then looked at Dev. "Is that a coincidence?"

Dev opened his mouth to argue, but knew it was pointless.

His uncle glanced at Eema and indicated down the corridor. "Don't let them out until this is over. You know the procedure." He turned around without another word and stepped back into the bunker.

Dev said nothing as Eema led them down the corridor to the canteen. He could hear Lot and Mason murmur with curiosity at every sealed door that they passed.

They entered the canteen, a vast room which could easily have sat their entire school. White tables and blue chairs filled the space. Soothing coloured lights switched automatically to soft pastel as the environment system analysed their mood, selecting a theme designed to calm them.

"Stay put," said Eema. Then she folded up into a ball and rolled back along the corridor the way they had come.

As Dev took a step towards the door it slid closed with a pneumatic hiss. He pressed the console pad next to it. It bleeped, but remained resolutely shut.

"Rats," Dev muttered under his breath. He closed his

eyes, his fingers moving in swirls over the console. Still nothing happened.

"What are you trying to do?" said Lot, looking at him curiously.

"The door is sealed. Unless I can get to the circuits I can't open it. Great!" Dev kicked the door out of frustration.

When he turned around he saw Lot had folded her arms, her brow furrowed as she stared at him. Mason sat quietly on the table behind her.

"OK, *Devon,* what is going on here? I came over because I felt sorry for you after my party. I wanted to try and be friends, but instead I have been shot at, survived being bludgeoned by a mechanical sheep, been kidnapped and taken into some weird underground lair, only to be imprisoned by rolling robot."

"Yeah, it's been an unusual day," said Dev, slumping down at a table. He stared sidelong at Mason. His uncle's comment about Mason and Lot appearing at the same time as the attack was bothering him.

Lot sucked in a long breath to calm herself. "Firstly, what is this place?"

Dev drummed his fingers on the table as he considered what he should say. What did he have to lose?

His uncle would be wiping their memories after this – his own too, with any luck.

"This is the Inventory. It's a warehouse for ... for really cool stuff."

"Like the military?" said Mason in a low voice.

"No. Well, yes. Sort of. Not just the military though. Inventors throughout the ages have created some amazing things you've never heard of. They still do. That's what we keep in here. It's mind-blowing stuff. You know, we have a car that runs entirely on water. No petrol, no oil – just water."

"So why keep it a secret?" asked Lot.

Dev shrugged. "I guess because some people think we're not ready for such responsibility."

Mason glanced up. "What people?"

Dev didn't even look at him. As far as he was concerned Mason was an unwelcome addition to a very unwelcome situation. "The World Consortium."

Mason and Lot exchanged baffled glances and shrugged.

"You've heard of the United Nations? Then they're ten levels above that."

"It sounds more like somebody would lose money," said Lot cynically. "Like the petrol companies."

"Maybe. But we have several water-powered cars down here. Cool, right? Problem is that we're running out of water too. Surely we need it to drink, not to use to run our cars. When something seems too good to be true, it usually is. Least that's what the World Consortium says. They own this place."

"Never heard of them," grumbled Mason.

Lot laughed. "That's because there's no such thing. He's playing with you."

Dev shook his head. "No, it's a real thing." Lot rolled her eyes, but Dev continued. "Everything here is secret. Top secret. In fact several levels above top secret."

Lot decided to humour him. "So that makes you a secret agent? Impressive."

Dev gave a jaded laugh. "I wish. More like an agent of secrets . . . or a caretaker. Junior caretaker," he added with a shake of the head. "My uncle runs the place. I . . . I just get in his way."

He thought he saw Lot soften for a moment, or perhaps it was just an illusion caused by the mood lighting. He couldn't be sure.

"The robot sheep are security, then?" said Lot.

"Decoys. We don't have time to run a real farm."

Mason stood up. "And the big wheelie robot?"

"Eema. She's the artificially intelligent computer system behind all of this." He gestured around the room. "The 'bot is just a husk that Eema downloads into, like a suit. She has different ones to do a bunch of different tasks. Like protecting us."

Lot began to pace the room. "Which brings me to question twenty-six. *Who* is attacking us?"

"And when can I go home?" Mason chipped in.

"Believe me, Mason, nobody wants you to leave here more than I do." Dev tried the door button again. It remained closed. "I suppose you can go the moment all of this is over."

Mason sat back down. His leg twitched nervously. He looked terrified. Dev was surprised to feel a little sympathy for him.

"And how long will that take?" asked Lot.

Dev shrugged. "Probably not long."

The Inventory had had intruders before, but they were usually people who had stumbled across the farm hoping to steal a few apples or, at worst, some farming machinery. Rogue foreign government agents had attacked the Inventory three times before, but those incursions hadn't lasted more than twenty minutes before they'd been seen off by security. This was the first time he'd seen such a large force attack. However, he was confident Eema and his uncle would stop them soon enough.

There was no way the invaders would ever set foot inside the Inventory.

THE ONLY WAY IS DOWN

Volta's electric screwdriver whirled as he assembled the last curved section from the packing box next to him. Once the final nuts were in place he gently laid the four-metre metal ring on the floor.

The Italian stepped aside as a wiry American mercenary began connecting thick cables to the ring.

"Why did that take you so long?" snarled the American.

"This is science – not Ikea!" barked Volta, but the American had turned away, trailing the cables back to a truck.

"Come on, people, we're losing time. Get the rig in place!" called Lee.

Lee watched as the American connected the cables to a large generator in the back of the truck. He glanced at his watch and anxiously chewed a stick of gum, aware that the Collector would be monitoring their progress from afar. They couldn't afford to fall behind schedule.

Four mercenaries, their uniforms sporting an entwined double-H logo, heaved the completed circle across the farm. A woman who went under the code name Fermi was marking an area of the ground with a laser.

"Place it within the markers. Quickly now!" She clapped her hands like an irritated schoolteacher.

Grunting, the mercenaries lowered the ring into place. She nodded to Lee. "We're ready."

Lee walked over to the edge of the ring as the generator hummed to life. The ring let out a hiss and the air within it shimmered like a heat haze.

"I hope you got your calculations right," Lee said to Fermi. "Otherwise we might just pour straight through the planet and off the edge of the earth."

The woman scowled. "Of course they're correct. I've calculated the osmotic pressure perfectly."

Lee activated his watch. The Collector's hologram appeared. "Sir, the portal is open."

"Be sure it works," snapped the Collector. "I don't want my assault team vaporized at the first hurdle." The image turned to face Volta. "You will jump first."

Volta paled. His eyes darted between his companions, all of whom avoided his gaze. "M-me?" he stammered.

"I need to know if it's safe," commanded the Collector, his voice lowered with menace. "Jump."

Lee watched a range of emotions cross the big Italian's face – from fear to determination. There was no hint of disobedience. They had all seen what the Collector could make men do, and none dared to defy him.

Volta tightened his weapon across his back and stood silently on the portal's rim. His eyes met Lee's for a moment – then he jumped into the shimmering energy field. Lee winced as the man was abruptly liquefied at an atomic level and accelerated into the ground with a wet splash.

Volta was passing through the earth by osmosis – meaning he could pass through dirt, stones, and even the atoms of the titanium lining of the Inventory's subterranean walls – before, in theory, snapping back together.

Lee and Kwolek waited as the rest of the team

assembled around the portal. Volta's voice suddenly crackled through the neutrino inner-ear headsets they all wore. "I'm through!" he cried with relief.

Lee smiled and sensed everybody was collectively catching their breath. It looked like they wouldn't die just yet.

The heist was on.

FIRST STEPS

Lot watched nervously as Dev paced the room. His anxiety was infectious. Lot was seriously regretting this visit. She had felt sorry for Dev since her party, and his quiet demeanour around school had always made her curious to know him better. But the drama of the attack on the farm and the revelation of the high-tech bunker beneath it was beginning to transform into anxiety and boredom. She wasn't enjoying being stuck in this huge empty room with nothing to do.

She watched as Dev tapped his peculiar watch and spoke into it.

"Eema, how much longer are we going to be stuck in

here? It's been an hour already."

There was no response. Lot saw Dev's frown deepen. She prided herself on being good at reading people's body language and often tried to analyse her parents. Her mother always told her off for trying to guess their moods. Lot suspected it was because she was mostly correct.

"Eema, come in. Uncle Parker?"

Again, a worrying silence.

"Is that normal?" said Mason, pulling his gaze away from his phone. "That they're ignoring you?"

Dev shook his head. "Even when my uncle's mad at me, he's always contactable. He doesn't trust me down here," he added as an afterthought.

Lot saw a flicker across Dev's face, one that hinted at loneliness, she thought. She was annoyed to find herself starting to feel sorry for him again, when really she should be angry.

Yet again, Dev tapped the door switch. It still didn't open.

"You've tried that before," Lot pointed out. "Do you expect it magically to start working?"

"Something's wrong. Something's very wrong," muttered Dev as he ran his fingers across the panel. Lot guessed that it must usually react to his handprint.

Dev thumped the wall. "The security system isn't responding. I should be able to open this!"

He accessed his watch using a series of small gestures across the screen. His eyes met Lot's and she saw him hesitate.

"I'm not really supposed to show anybody this." Dev sighed and made the final gesture. A holographic map of the complex floated over the watch, expanding five times the size of the screen.

Lot's eyes widened in astonishment. She had seen all kinds of neat technology on the aircraft her father flew – but this was obviously much more advanced.

"WOW!" howled Mason as he peered up from his own phone. "That is so cool!"

"Simple holographic projection. Years out of date," said Dev as he spun the map around with one finger and located the canteen at the edge. Even on this security map, the inner rooms of the Inventory were missing for the sake of secrecy.

"Is this where we are?" Lot pointed. She was determined not to sound too impressed with the technology Dev had at his fingertips.

"Uh-huh. And I should be able to access most of

the cameras from here." He tapped tiny holographic representations of the surveillance cameras dotted about the map. Each time a small window popped open showing a video feed. Each one was blank.

"Are they broken?" Lot asked.

Dev shook his head. "Unlikely."

Mason stood up and joined them. "Then maybe it's time we got out of here and saw for ourselves?" He examined the door switch panel.

"Oh, sure," scoffed Dev. "We'll just hack into the security and override the lock mechanism—"

Mason kicked the panel with his steel-plated toecap. The metal plate buckled, then fell from the clips that held it in place. Before Dev could protest, Mason had pulled two wires off the circuit inside and twisted them together. There was a spark – then the door swished open.

Lot looked at him quizzically. "How did you do that?"

Mason's cheeks flushed. "My brother taught me how to hot-wire a car ignition a couple of times..."

Lot raised an eyebrow at Dev. "So much for your super security systems."

Dev walked wordlessly out of the canteen and

glanced around the corridor. Everything appeared normal. Quiet. He closed the map on his watch and tried the communicator again. "Eema, Uncle Parker, do you read me?"

Nothing. He began to walk back the way they had come, beckoning the others to follow. "Keep close."

The corridor curved sharply as they drew near to the command bunker. The bleak corridors reminded Lot of the many military installations she had visited with her father. The first couple of doors they passed were closed – but Dev tensed and stopped in his tracks when he saw three were not only open, but the contents of the rooms had been thrown out into the corridor.

"My uncle is a tidiness freak," he explained. "He would go crazy over a mess like this."

Lot felt her fingers bunch into fists as she realized what Dev was implying. "That means somebody else is in here, doesn't it?"

Dev nodded and slowly moved forward. Lot kept close, noticing Mason was trailing behind. *Not so tough now,* she thought.

The first doorway was obstructed by a large metal shelf that had been toppled into the corridor. Boxes of electrical components had burst open, scattering their contents across the floor: reels of different-sized wire gauges, rods, pneumatic pumps, electric motors, soldering irons and other mechanical pieces.

They froze when he heard laughter coming from the next room.

"Down!" hissed Dev, as he ducked behind the fallen shelf.

Lot and Mason crushed behind him just as two men emerged from the room. They were muscular, and from their profiles they looked like identical twins. Both had rifles slung over their backs. Not primitive guns, Lot noticed. They were some kind of alternative advanced weapon that oozed menace. She spotted an entwined double-H logo on their uniforms.

"And they said security here was the best in the world! Ha!" scoffed one man.

"They hadn't counted on the Wright brothers!" said the other, raising his fist so the other could bump it. They continued down the corridor, disappearing from view as it curved. "This Iron Fist better be worth it."

"Do you know them?" whispered Mason.

"Never seen them before in my life," said Dev, his mind racing. "They shouldn't be here." He slowly stood up.

Lot grabbed his hand to pull him back. "Wait!

Where are you going?"

"I want to know what they were doing in there. Judging by the mess, they were looking for something."

Dev peered around the door frame to check there was nobody else waiting in the room. Coast clear, he slipped inside. Lot hurried after him. She glanced back at Mason, who tried to mask his apprehension.

"I'll keep watch," he said.

The room was filled with aging stationery items. Paper clips had begun to rust, while pages of writing pads had turned yellow. She supposed that if the Inventory was so high-tech the stationery had gone unused for decades.

A cupboard had been pulled away from the wall and the concrete surface beyond had been split open by sledgehammers, which had been thrown aside with the rest of the rubble. The cavity that had been revealed housed a series of plastic pipes that had been sliced open, revealing a thick trunk of wires. They all had crocodile clips attached, while the mass of fibre optic cables had small prisms attached to bounce the light signal within. The hijacking wires ran to a laptop that sat to one side of the space. The heavy-duty casing around the laptop was the kind used by soldiers during military operations.

"They've tapped into your security system," said Mason from the doorway.

Lot jumped. She hadn't been expecting him to follow them inside. "How do you know that?" she said.

"Duh! Have you never seen a film?"

Dev edged past Lot and tapped the laptop's touchpad. The screen flicked to life with a series of windows. Each was labelled – radio, microwave, video, optics, audio – and showed sine waves pulsing up and down. "That's why I can't raise Eema," he said. "They're intercepting everything. But if I just unplug—"

He reached for a clip – but Lot grabbed his hand. "OK, genius. How do you know that's the right one?"

Dev smiled. "Trust me, it's . . . a skill of mine."

Lot hesitated for a moment, then let him go. There was a confidence in his smile that she hadn't seen before.

Dev ran his fingers over the wires, a frown of concentration on his forehead.

Lot and Mason exchanged a curious look. "I don't think massaging the wires is going to help," Mason quipped.

Dev's brow furrowed. Then he shook his head. "It's not working."

"What's not working?" asked Lot.

"He thinks he's some kind of rubbish superhero," said Mason.

"I'll unplug them all."

"And they will know we're here!" said Mason suddenly.

Lot nodded. "He's right. We need to get to the surface and raise the alarm." She didn't like the look on Dev's face. "We *can* raise the alarm . . . can't we?"

Dev looked between her and Mason. "Not exactly."

Lot felt her heart sink. She wasn't claustrophobic, but the idea of being trapped underground and never seeing daylight again sent a chill down her spine.

"I wouldn't know who to call," Dev explained. "It's not like we can ask the police for help. They don't know this facility exists."

"The military?" asked Lot hopefully. "Maybe my dad—"

Dev shook his head. "Like I said, the Inventory goes beyond stupid things like countries. The World Consortium is above all that."

Mason groaned. "You must have a number? Somebody you call when you need help. If they're that important we can just dial 'one', surely?"

"We're not the kind of place that usually needs help," said Dev. "Besides, I don't exactly have a direct phone number for the World Consortium."

"Brilliant!" spat Mason. "So what do we do?"

"First, we do everything we can to spoof the security."

Dev held up his watch and, using the tiny embedded camera, took photos of Mason and Lot. Lot watched as Dev transferred them wirelessly to the network.

"Is that it?" Mason asked incredulously. "We need a real plan!"

Lot silently agreed. She saw Dev's shoulders sag.

"The only person who could help is my uncle. And I have no idea where he is right now."

WE'RE WATCHING YOU

Somewhere far from the Inventory a message appeared on a screen. There were no alarms, no flashing warning lights, nothing that indicated the magnitude of the problem that had been detected.

The plastic coffee cup that had been placed on the desk lasted a whole six seconds before the figure who had just placed it there read the message on screen, and knocked it over as they sprinted from the room.

The unthinkable was happening right now.

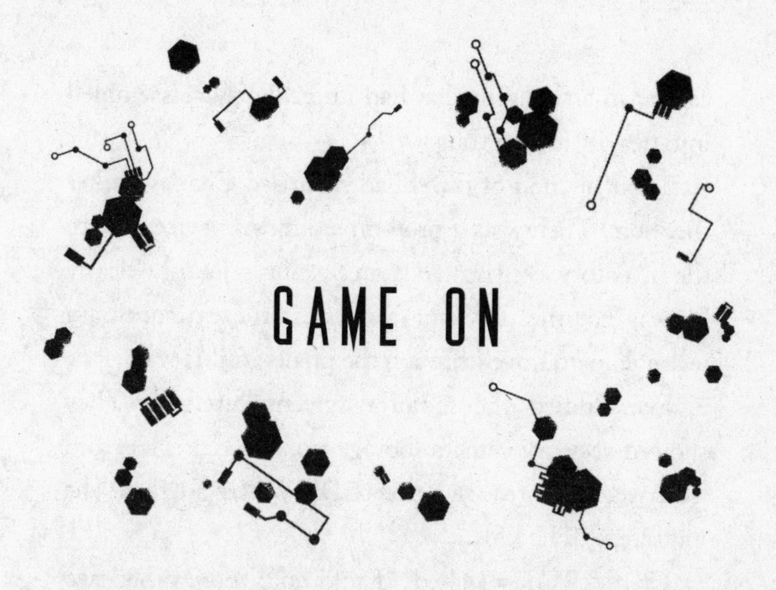

GAME ON

Charles Parker strained at his cuffs. They didn't budge, not that he had expected them to. The electromagnetic band around his wrist allowed his captors to loosen them with ease if they required him to do anything – or tighten them if he was being annoying. He slumped back in his chair.

The attack on the Inventory had come with a vicious suddenness that had taken Charles by surprise. One moment he had been monitoring the situation from the bunker as he and Eema had frantically tried to intercept the assailants' signals. The next moment an entire assault team had literally oozed through the bunker's ceiling in a fine rain that had immediately reassembled into heavily armed thugs.

Their method of travel had surprised Charles Parker the most. There was a prototype osmosis device here in the Inventory, confiscated from a genius scientist. Clearly he was not the only one to possess the extraordinary technology to travel through the planet in this way.

Lee studied the monitor screens carefully. They showed security camera footage from the corridors and lower-security areas in perfect 3D. "Where are they?" he muttered. "The kids."

Charles Parker sighed. "I told you, those other two children shouldn't have been here in the first place. But they can cause you no harm while you fruitlessly attempt to infiltrate the complex."

"We got this far, didn't we?"

"The Inventory has long proved to be impregnable, even from the *inside*."

Lee smiled amiably. "Well, if you simply open up access to the Red Zone for us, then we can get out of your hair."

Despite the danger, Charles Parker laughed and shook his head. "You know that's simply not possible. And you can't use your osmosis trick on any of the vault walls. The gravity field between them could shred atoms apart. And the doors. . ."

"I am aware of the problems ahead," said Lee. "But my boss wants what's in there. And he does tend to get what he wants . . . one way or another."

"Your boss? And who might that be?"

Lee knelt down and met Charles's gaze. "He goes by the name of the Collector."

Charles Parker felt his blood run cold. The mere mention of the name was enough to raise the hairs on the back of his neck.

Lee's smile broadened when he saw its effect. "Oh, you've heard of him?" Lee playfully ruffled Charles's hair and moved back to his seat. "So you know what he's capable of?" Charles dared not answer. Lee turned his attention back to the monitors. "So getting to the Red Zone will be difficult, but not impossible. Yet that is what we do, isn't it, Charles? The *impossible*. Even if it means losing a few lives?"

Charles Parker's eyes narrowed and his voice dropped to a whisper. "Do not think for a moment that your threats have any effect upon me." His voice dropped further. "Your orders are not to harm me, correct?"

Lee's silence confirmed this.

Suddenly Lee spotted something on the monitor and frowned. "Hey, Volta, I've got something here!" he called to his colleague.

Volta ran into the room and looked at the screen. "What am I supposed to see?" he asked.

Lee pointed to the window showing an angle of the empty canteen. "This." He paused, then looked expectantly at Volta. "Do you see it?"

Volta shook his head. "I see a door."

Lee sighed and rewound the image, then zoomed in on the door. Again, nobody could be seen – but the lock on the door suddenly broke and dropped to the floor as if struck by a ghost. Moments later the door opened . . . then slid closed again.

"They're *invisible*?" said Volta.

Lee shrugged. "It seems so, but how . . . that's another matter. The twins checked in. The external lines are secure. The surface team is ready and Eema has been partitioned offline. We have complete control, so why don't you go and do your thing, huh? It's game on."

The look of hatred Volta threw at Lee was not lost on Charles. Obviously the big mercenary hated taking orders from him. Volta wordlessly hurried from the room.

Lee slowly turned to Charles Parker and steepled his fingers. "Y'know, I was instructed not to harm you. Those kids, on the other hand. . ."

Charles Parker's eyes darted across the monitors as he wondered just what his nephew was up to. . .

YELLOW ZONE

Dev ran down the corridor with Lot and Mason close behind. Lot eyed the surveillance cameras they passed under. "Are you sure they can't see us?" she asked.

"Where are we going?" Mason added.

"Don't worry about the cameras," said Dev. "I've taken care of them." *At least I hope so,* he added to himself. He had used the same trick many times on Eema and just hoped that the intruders hadn't worked out what was happening. "And we are heading somewhere safe."

"Wait," said Mason, "shouldn't we try and get out? You know, very far from the men with weapons?"

"It's not going to take them long to find us in these

corridors," Lot added. "And there's nowhere to hide."

They turned a corner and Dev stopped at a large circular door that looked more like a bank vault.

"Exactly," said Dev. "That's why we're going to hide in the warehouse until help arrives. They'll never find us in there. The place is a labyrinth."

He placed his hand on a black plate in the centre of the door. It not only scanned his palm, but also checked his DNA: foolproof security that meant only he and his uncle could access the room beyond.

The door rolled open and the trio entered the cavernous room beyond.

"That was easy," said Lot.

"When I was on the network before, I instructed the computer to let me in." Dev smiled. "Why make things any more difficult than they have to be?"

"Wow," said Mason for the umpteenth time that day as they entered the Yellow Zone.

The space was huge. A curved roof spanned some four storeys above them, while lines of shelving formed many avenues that obscured the distant walls.

Lot was impressed. "It looks like the world's biggest DIY store."

Mason's foot tapped the wide coloured stripes painted on the floor, fanning out in separate directions. "Where do these go?"

"The colours indicate different sections within this zone and then lead on to even bigger zones, each more secure than the last. Even I can't get into some of them. Not that we have to because we're going to hide right here. This is the minimum-security vault. It's all category one stuff in here."

Lot ran across to the nearest shelf and pulled down a large bell jar. It was filled with multicoloured balls. She read the label. "Hyperballs?"

"Don't touch *anything*," Dev snapped.

Lot already had her hand in the jar and pulled out a red ball. "Relax," she sighed. "What do you take me for? And I was starting to think you were cool."

The comment threw Dev for a moment. Nobody had ever called him cool. He reached for the ball, but Lot pulled away tutting.

"Be careful! It's hyper-inertia perpetual silicon," he exclaimed.

Lot blinked. "Wow. Geek-speak overload." She bounced it on the floor.

Dev lunged forward to stop her – but missed. "NO!"

The ball bounced from the floor at an angle and instantly gained speed. It ricocheted from a supporting shelf, now travelling twice as fast. It rebounded from another shelf and whooshed between Dev and Lot with the sound of a bullet, forcing them to recoil.

Lot watched in astonishment as the ball *poing*ed from surface to surface, each time building momentum. They eventually lost track of it down the maze of aisles.

"Sorry," Lot said with her best *don't-hate-me* smile.

Dev gently took the jar from her hands and placed it back on the shelf. "Each bounce increases its velocity, building it to a critical mass. Then it's like a wrecking ball. That's why they were banned in 1963 when a kid threw a whole box out of a window and demolished a skyscraper."

"I never heard about that," said Lot, trying to keep her voice sounding apologetic.

"Exactly. Everything in here was banned, confiscated or hidden for a reason. And a lot of serious people with very *serious* attitudes spent a lot of *serious* money to keep it all quiet. Everything is dangerous."

A huge clatter made them spin around. Mason had accidentally knocked over a pile of metal sheets. He looked pale, frozen to the spot, as if he expected them to explode.

"It was an accident!" he yelped, starting back. "What are these things?" His eyes searched the smooth metal surface for any clue.

Dev rolled his eyes. "They're spare shelves, genius. Now will you two..." He trailed off as a harsh buzz sounded from the door behind.

"What was that?" asked Mason, backing towards Dev, his eyes trained on the door.

"Somebody's trying to get in," whispered Dev.

"Can they?" asked Lot in a low voice.

The textbook answer was *no way*, but the infiltrators had already entered the complex itself, which was supposed to be impossible.

Impossible . . . so how had they done it?

Dev studied Lot and Mason. "Why did you come to the farm today?"

Both Lot and Mason exchanged a look, unsure which of them Dev was addressing. An uncomfortable moment passed by before either of them spoke.

Lot shrugged. "I wanted to spend more time with you. Get to know you."

"After *years* of ignoring me in school?"

Lot folded her arms, her chin tilting up defiantly. "You ignored *me* – get it right."

Dev had no comeback to that. Instead he nodded to Mason. "And you?"

"I told you. I wanted . . . I wanted to pick on you." He continued quickly when he saw Dev's eyes narrow. "You're an easy target. Makes me look good." He hung his head in shame. "I was being an idiot, OK?"

"Give me one reason I shouldn't just leave you behind," said Dev.

"Dev!" Lot gasped.

Dev kept his eyes locked with Mason's, searching for any hint of hostility. "Why not? He'd do the same to me."

Mason met his gaze . . . then shrugged. "I can't think of a reason," he said miserably.

"Dev, we're wasting time!" snapped Lot.

Dev expected a thrill for finally pulling one over on Mason, but instead he felt guilty. He refused to meet Lot's gaze and turned his attention instead to the nearby shelves. "Can you guys skateboard?"

"Sure," said Lot.

Mason didn't look so confident. "I have. I mean, y'know, when I was younger."

Dev dashed to the shelf and pulled three skateboards off it. He flicked a switch on each and they clattered to the floor in a row.

Mason regarded them with suspicion. "I don't know, man. There seem to be a few wheels missing."

He was right. Instead of the traditional four wheels, there was just one big orb poking through the centre of the board, with footpads at the front and back. Dev had tossed them carelessly to the floor, but the boards remained perfectly level.

"OmniBoards," explained Dev. "Just like a Segway – it's almost impossible to fall off." He saw their expressions. "You have ridden Segways before, right?"

Lot and Mason exchanged a look and shrugged.

BOOM! The vault door suddenly trembled as it was struck from behind. Dev watched in fascination as the metal started to turn white at the centre. Frost. The cold slowly radiated outwards with a cracking sound.

Dev jumped on to a board and stood, perfectly balanced. "Just lean in whichever direction you want to travel. It's time we—"

Another bang resounded through the hangar as the super-chilled surface of the vault door suddenly shattered like glass as it was hammered from behind.

Soldiers, led by a powerfully built woman with red hair, began scrambling through the gap and spotted them immediately.

"There they are!"

Lot and Mason didn't need telling twice. They jumped on to their boards, arms windmilling crazily to keep their balance – not that they needed to; the boards immediately corrected for their weight and remained stationary.

Mason leaned forward, propelling his board towards a shelf with a surprising turn of speed. He yelled, arms covering his face as he instinctively tried to lean away from the collision. The board's single-orb wheel responded instantly and he swerved aside, travelling ninety degrees in the opposite direction. He screamed with delight, his arms extended like a tightrope walker to keep his balance.

Dev and Lot drifted either side of him. Despite the present danger, they couldn't wipe the grins off their faces.

There was a bass-heavy pulsing noise, then a bolt of shimmering air passed their heads and struck a shelf close to them, which exploded with a hollow boom.

"Sonic weapons!" yelled Dev, instantly recognizing

the technology. He glanced behind to see two of their pursuers tracking them with their weapons.

More shots followed in rapid succession. Dev swerved out of the way of one, colliding into Mason, who veered sideways as he flailed for balance. It was a manoeuvre that saved his life, as the second sonic blast detonated just in front of him.

"Come on!" Dev led the way down an aisle that took them out of the line of fire. As he did so, he noticed the other attackers running forward, the soles of their boots glowing with each step until they were suddenly lifted centimetres off the ground and were moving as if on ice. They were closing in fast.

The frictionless boots were *way* better than the clunky HoverBoots, thought Dev. It took all his concentration to pull his gaze from the impressive technology and take in the pursers themselves.

One was a grim-faced man with the muscular build of a professional soldier. The other was the woman with long red hair and a mean-looking metallic exoskeleton, more advanced than Dev had ever seen before.

"Follow me," he urged the others. A volley of sonic bolts overhead forced him to duck. One was so close that his ears popped.

"They're catching up," yelled Lot as she risked a look behind.

They took a corner at speed, boxes crashing from the shelves in their wake. Dozens of banned handheld gadgets cascaded across the floor. The pursuing mercenaries swerved aside.

Dev cursed under his breath. He wished he had a pack of Prism-Buddies; they were exactly what he needed right now. But unlike secret agents in the movies, who conveniently always had the right gadget to hand, Dev was surrounded by everything he *didn't* need.

Still. . .

He veered closer to the shelf unit and randomly swiped a box as he passed. A military stencil across the lid warned: CAUTION! PORTABLE HOLE.

Keeping his eyes on the path ahead – and ducking as another blast shot overhead – Dev's fingers gouged open the cardboard. He pulled out a large gel pack that felt squidgy in his hand. Suspended between the transparent layers was a large black circle.

"Seriously weird," said Dev.

Steadying his balance, he peeled the gel layer off and, careful not to touch the device itself, threw the black disc behind him.

The disc seemed to expand as it soared into the path of his pursuers. They were travelling so fast that two of them were unable to avoid it and simply vanished through the vertical hole. The hole then folded up on itself and disappeared with a tiny pop. Dev tore his gaze away. It was best not to ponder too much on the fate of the soldiers. It was more important that they escaped – and that meant out-thinking the remaining mercenaries.

"Next right!" commanded Dev.

In this section the shelves suddenly petered out, replaced by barrels and long tubes, all part of some colossal spider-like machine that dated back to the 1800s. Dev had never quite figured out why some madman had invented it in the first place.

"There's no cover here, you idiot!" Mason barked.

"Wanna bet?" said Dev – and veered suddenly into a long tube that had formed a monstrous mechanical leg. Lot and Mason only just managed to follow. Mason ducked to avoid cracking his head on the side of the pipe.

Both of the skating pursuers rolled in after them.

The tube was twice Dev's height – perfect for what he had in mind. "Just do what I do," he said. He crouched, then angled his body. Lot and Mason followed suit –

just as their pursuers opened fire again.

Dev led the way as they corkscrewed up one side of the tube, across the ceiling and down the other.

"Kwolek! Shoot the boards!" the man yelled. Sonic bolts tore holes in the side of the tube as their pursuers followed in a similar corkscrew motion.

"No!" Kwolek screamed.

It was too late. Kwolek managed to avoid the hole that her colleague had created, but the man couldn't deviate from his spiralling path and slipped straight through it. His momentum was so great that he soared from the tube a full ten metres before slamming hard into a shelf with a splat they could all hear.

The towering shelving unit wobbled precariously, then came crashing down on top of the mercenary, dozens of gizmos pinning him to the floor.

The three children shot from the other end of tube at speed.

Dev led his companions in another tight turn, returning to the cover offered by more tall shelves.

Lot glanced behind as she drew alongside him. "I can't see her. Do you think she's given up?"

An explosion tore the ground just ahead of them. Leaning into their OmniBoards, the three kids veered aside just in time. Dev turned and saw the snarling woman was gaining on them.

"I think it's time we caught some air!" Dev leaned his entire weight forward, pushing the OmniBoard for every jot of speed. Lot and Mason saw where Dev was leading them, and their mouths sagged open in shock.

"No way!" screamed Mason.

A wild volley of sonic bolts blasted around them. Luckily Kwolek couldn't steady her aim as she skated. She was too engrossed in her targets to notice what lay beyond them—

A four-storey drop.

At the bottom of the vertical drop was an area populated by even bigger shelves that held a series of aircraft and vehicles.

Dev, Lot and Mason rolled over the black-and-yellow hazard marking on the margin of the pit and soared off the edge.

There was nothing they could do. A fall from this height and speed would easily kill them.

But Dev's aim had been perfect. They landed on the top of a shelving rack teetering precariously four storeys above the hangar floor. While his aim was good, his landing wasn't. He stumbled and the OmniBoard slipped from under his feet and shot off the ledge.

Dev rolled helplessly across the shelf and felt a sharp pain as Lot, then Mason, both barrelled into him. They too were pitched off their boards and slid to a halt, crushed against him.

Dev sat upright in time to see Kwolek skid to a halt at the edge of the pit. She tracked the noise of the OmniBoards clattering to the ground below, before her gaze snapped back up to see her targets scrambling around the fuselage of a helicopter, one of several, stacked on the shelving unit that had saved them. She fired her sonic rifle at them, but the shots merely tore holes in the side of a chopper as the trio ducked out of sight.

Dev heard her bellow with rage. He risked peeking from his cover. Kwolek was sucking in a deep breath to yell an insult just as the Hyperball Lot had thrown ricocheted from a shelving stack and struck her in the chest with such force that she was hurled backwards against a rack. Her head lolled as she fell unconscious.

NOW I SEE YOU

Lee's fist slammed down on the computer keyboard. The force of the blow still didn't change the flashing warning box on the screen.

ACCESS DENIED!

He turned to Charles Parker. "There must be an override password."

"There is," Charles replied casually. He raised his cuffs, indicating he needed them relaxed. Lee used an app on his phone to weaken the electromagnetic force between the handcuffs, allowing Charles to stretch his arms.

"Ah, much better." Charles typed a lengthy password, a combination of numbers, letters both upper and lower case, and a host of punctuation symbols. He hit enter and the message flashed:

PASSWORD EXPIRED.

Charles Parker shrugged. "I did warn you. Once the alarm system is triggered, majestic level passwords are automatically scrambled. It takes *days* to reset them."

Lee studied the screen – the entry for IRON FIST was visible, but the contents of the file remained tantalizingly out of reach.

Charles Parker leaned over his shoulder. "So that's what the Collector is after?"

Before Lee could reply, an apprehensive mercenary entered the room. "We have a small problem."

"You can't find the kids?"

"Well, actually we *did* find them. But they escaped. We have three men down and Kwolek was knocked out."

"Kids took three of your guys down?" said Lee incredulously.

"They were hiding in the Yellow Zone and things . . . just got out of hand. The rest of the team have pushed through the zone and are proceeding to up the Blue Zone."

Lee raised his arm and reached for his watch, but a thought made him hesitate.

"I wonder what your boss will say when he discovers a bunch of children have outsmarted you," said Charles Parker in his best mocking tones.

Lee lowered his arm. "Send a couple of men to sweep the warehouse for those brats. You have them cornered, so it shouldn't be too difficult."

"Yes, sir." The soldier nodded and exited.

Lee wagged a finger at the monitors. "If you had cameras in the main zones you would have made my life a whole lot easier."

Charles shrugged. "Why would I want to do that?"

Lee shook his head and turned back to his laptop. A window displayed lines of dense coding which he began to trawl through.

"I got no idea why he wanted you kept alive," Lee muttered.

If Charles Parker responded, Lee didn't hear – he had suddenly noticed something in the code. "Well, I'll be deleted . . . what do we have here?"

He spun the screen so Charles could see. "This is

deep in Eema's security algorithms." He highlighted a section of the code. It took him a moment to realize that Charles Parker had no clue what he was looking at. "This code shouldn't be here. It's malware – a Trojan. Y'know, like a virus?"

"Impossible!" snapped Charles. "These systems are protected from the outside world and run on a *completely new* type of computer code. They are immune from viruses, worms and Trojans."

"Nevertheless," said Lee with a smirk. "You're looking at one right here. It's a real doozy. It tells the cameras to ignore whatever image is held on the three encrypted pictures stored within the Trojan itself. I can't access them, but I bet they're photographs of the kids taken on their phones. As soon as the security cameras identify them, this Trojan code paints them out of the image in real time! That's why we couldn't see them when I played back the footage from the canteen! Genius! It means they could be standing in front of any camera right now and we wouldn't see them."

"Devon!" Charles exclaimed, shaking his head. "I could never work out how he bypassed Eema and sneaked around the complex."

"Your kid's a first-rate coder," said Lee, genuinely impressed. "He even fooled Eema's artificial intelligence."

"He's not my *kid*," Charles said on a low voice. For a moment his eyes drifted away from the code on the screen and he seemed to be thinking about something else entirely. He caught Lee looking at him curiously and snapped out of his reverie. He stretched his arms to get the blood circulating again. "Three children have outwitted not only your finest troops, but you too. Such a shame."

Lee punched a button on his mobile phone and Charles's magnetic cuffs immediately went to full power – snapping his hands painfully together in front of him.

Charles slumped back in his chair. "You are mistaken if you think Devon will just be hiding in there, hoping you won't find him. By now he probably already knows that you're looking for Iron Fist." Charles enjoyed the worried look on Lee's face. "He'll take the initiative and will be plotting to stop you. And he's more than one step ahead. . ."

A TERRIBLE PLAN

"So what's the plan?" Lot asked in a low voice.

"Hide." Dev made sure to use his best matter-of-fact voice. "And we get as far away from those creeps as possible. Whatever they're looking for, I don't want to know."

They had scrambled along the shelving stack, inching around one helicopter fuselage after another. The scrapped advanced prototype machines were so big they barely fitted on the shelving space even with their rotors swept back and tied in place with heavy cables. Each vehicle was slightly different – a larger canopy, corkscrewed rotors or bulging weapon pods. In places there was hardly any space to squeeze past and they had to be careful where they placed their feet. Dev loathed heights and he felt his pulse quicken and his palms turn sweaty every time he looked down.

Midway along the shelf they came across a ladder bolted to the side of the stack. It stretched to the shelf below. Dev found that even scarier. It was an open ladder with no safety cage, nothing to stop them plummeting to their deaths. In all his time at the Inventory he had never explored the high shelves. He had been up once or twice with his uncle using a cherry-picker crane, but he hadn't felt safe even in the relative comfort of the crane's basket.

Still, it was the only way down.

The moment they descended to the third level, Dev had to sit down to stop his legs from shaking. This shelf was filled with drones and yet more helicopters; these, however, didn't have rotors. Some had giant fans bolted to their sides, while others had more delicate and revolutionary engines constructed from a fine web of wires.

"These are incredible," said Lot, impressed. She ran a hand along a fuselage. She had been around aircraft her whole life but had never seen anything like this.

"I wish we could just start one up and fly out of here," Dev said, closing his eyes in an attempt to calm himself.

"I could probably fly it," said Lot. Dev wasn't surprised to see she was serious. "My dad took me up for a few lessons in a training chopper. It's easy . . . well, after a while it is."

Mason sniggered. "Is there nothing you can't do?"

Lot looked thoughtful. "My dad always says there's nothing you can't do if you try hard enough. He always says, 'Lot, you keep flying high.'" She smiled – a smile that quickly faded. She hoped she'd live long enough to see him again.

"We just need to keep low and stay quiet," said Dev flatly.

"And who will come to rescue us?" said Mason. The OmniBoard chase had left him sullen and subdued. Dev could tell he was frightened, but didn't have the heart to taunt him. Like it or not, he and his nemesis were stuck together for now.

"And what about your uncle?" said Lot.

Dev felt a twinge of guilt that they hadn't even attempted to check if his uncle was safe, but *he* was the one who'd imprisoned them in the canteen. He was sure

Charles Parker was more than capable of looking after himself.

The faint rumble of an engine got their attention, but from their vantage point they could see nothing. Lot and Mason looked at Dev expectantly, and reluctantly he realized that they were looking to him for leadership.

Taking a deep breath, and ignoring his shaking legs, Dev swung out on to the ladder and climbed halfway up to get a better view. From there he could just see movement between the distant aisles across the warehouse.

"It's a tank," he breathed.

"A tank?" Lot echoed. "Are they going to shoot our hiding place apart?"

The heavy war machine passed deeper into the hangar. Dev couldn't make out the model, but there were dozens of them in storage. "I bet they're using it to break into the next zone. This isn't just an ordinary heist; they're ignoring most of the things in here. They're looking for something *specific.*"

"Iron Fist," said Mason suddenly. "That's what those guys back in the corridor were talking about. What is it?"

Dev shook his head. "Never heard of it. Then again, I

have no idea what's really in here. I don't even think my uncle knows. This place has been around for a *long* time."

"How long?" asked Lot.

"I think President Washington and Prime Minister Pitt the Younger started off the World Consortium . . . so that was, um, way back." Dev's grasp of history was thin at the best of times and he was now regretting not having listened during lessons. Finally history might have a use. "Anyway, whatever Iron Fist is, they're going to have a lot of trouble getting to it."

"But what if they do?"

"They won't."

Lot folded her arms and looked insistently at him. "But what if they do? They have a tank now, after all. Are we talking end of the world type stuff?"

Dev was about to laugh off the suggestion, but couldn't muster the will to deceive her. He knew how dangerous some of the items were. It wasn't inconceivable that there was a doomsday machine deep inside the Inventory. In fact, when he thought about it, he realized there could be dozens of world-ending machines in here. Keeping that kind of power out of people's hands was the purpose of the Inventory, after all.

He shrugged.

Mason looked thoughtful. "How big is this place?"

Dev opened an art app on his watch and the holographic image expanded over his arm. He drew a series of three interlocking circles resembling half the Olympic symbol.

"OK, these are the three main corridors. There are dormitories, the canteen, general storage areas, workshops and repair facilities. It was originally designed to house hundreds of staff, now there's just the two of us. And Eema."

"A fat lot of good your security has been," sniffed Lot. "All Eema managed was to lock us in a room. And even that was easy to get out of, thanks to Mase."

Mason blushed at the compliment.

Dev didn't reply. Eema's ineffectiveness had been bothering him. He drew a large box at the bottom of the circles. "This is the Yellow Zone we are in now. It's designed to allow access through the roof." He pointed to a colossal closed door in the roof above, like the sliding roofs in sporting stadiums, only on a much grander scale. "There are a couple of those. And platforms like this are raised and lowered so vehicles could be brought down."

Lot realized the pit they were in made sense. It was

actually a colossal elevator that could rise up to ground level. At the moment the platform had been lowered down, just like a mechanic's pit.

"So why don't we just switch the elevator on and go up?" asked Mason.

"Because it takes hours to get to the roof, by which time the guys with guns could have stopped for a coffee, got a haircut, then strolled over and caught us. Besides, the controls are back in the command bunker." He tapped a tiny dot on one of the corridor rings.

Dev added another two boxes following on from the Yellow Zone. "Through the next door is the Blue Zone. Much higher security. I've only been in there a few times myself. Beyond that – well, I have no idea just how many rooms there are and what the layout is. I know the Red Zone is somewhere down here. That's one of the places I'm forbidden from entering."

"Why?" asked Lot.

"My uncle always told me it was 'need to know' security."

Lot smiled. "And let me guess. He thought you didn't *need to know*?" She met Dev's gaze and must have read the unhappiness there because her expression softened. "It must have been very lonely growing up here."

Dev nodded. He wasn't used to having anybody he could talk to. Letting off steam usually involved shouting at Eema, and it was impossible to check if the bodiless artificial intelligence was paying attention.

"Why don't we just ask your computer for help?" said Mason, pointing at Dev's watch.

Dev shot him an annoyed look. "Because, genius, Eema's not responding. I bet they're blocking the Wi-Fi."

"But you put our pictures on that Trojan virus of yours," Lot pointed out. "You managed to get into the system then."

"That's because they had hardwired their laptop straight into the network."

Lot smiled. "Then why don't we?" She pointed up to the ceiling another four storeys above them. Catwalks stretched precariously overhead. They were there in case maintenance needed to be carried out on the air-conditioning conduits and masses of wiring that ran across the warehouse. "I can see a whole bunch of cables," she pointed out.

Dev started to feel a glimmer of hope – but it was extinguished when reality caught up with him. "There's no way we can get up there. The access ladders are against the walls and they'll see us coming."

"We don't need a *ladder*," said Lot as she tapped his forehead with her finger. "We need imagination."

"Sure. We'll just pull out one of the engines out of a chopper and float right up," Dev laughed.

He stopped when he saw Lot's face. She was being serious.

SMART DOORS

The mercenary stared at the door ahead of them. It was twice the size of the portal they'd frozen and shattered to gain access to the Yellow Zone. He reached out to touch the smooth cobalt-blue surface – but Fermi yanked his hand away.

"Don't touch it," she warned. "The doors are made from smart materials. The adaptive security system knows we froze and shattered the last door, so. . ."

She pulled a water bottle from a clip on her belt and squirted it at the door. The water froze the instant it touched the surface, the entire arc of water solidifying, right back to the neck of the bottle, which she snatched away before the bottle froze too.

"I would've lost my fingers!" the mercenary said in alarm.

"At the very least. The adaptive security won't let us use the same trick twice."

"If it's like ice, we can smash through it."

Fermi shook her head. "Uh-uh. It's cold. Not brittle. We're going to need something that packs a punch."

She turned to look at the tank that was slowly driving towards them.

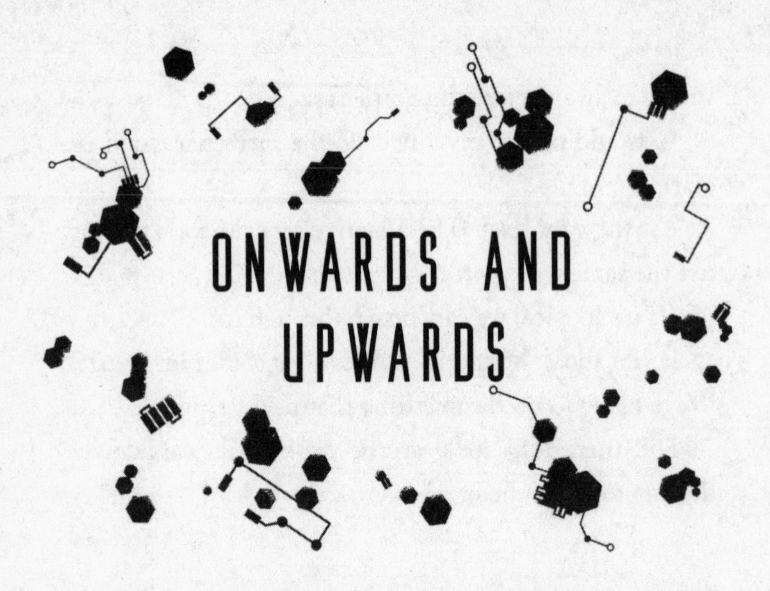

ONWARDS AND UPWARDS

"This is a bad idea," said Dev for the fifth time.

"I totally agree," said Mason nervously.

"Quit complaining and give me a hand," said Lot as she kicked the end of a wrench to unfasten the last bolt holding the engine in place. Two solid aims and the bolt finally began to turn.

It had taken an assortment of tools, lifted from the numerous toolboxes mounted to every shelf in the Inventory, to get this far. Once the stubborn bolt was out, the three of them lifted the turbine from the stubby aircraft's wing. Lot had wanted them to try to fly the entire craft, but Dev pointed to a red tag on the other engine indicating that it was broken.

The machine they now held was circular, about the size of a coffee table, and surprisingly light. Dev had selected the small two-seater craft, as he knew this was one of a range that employed silent engine technology; the engines were made from a lattice of wires held in a circular frame rather than from noisy moving parts. A high-voltage electric current was passed through them and, by some bizarre quirk of physics, the ionized air lifted the engine. It was a cheap, efficient technology, but because scientists decided it couldn't work without rewriting a few lines of physics, it was thrown into the Inventory.

"How do you know about these?" said Lot. In all the time spent with her father at military bases, she had never seen the likes of this before.

"IonoCraft are cool," said Dev with a shrug. "I used to make them out of spare parts all the time. Thomas Townsend Brown invented them in the 1920s and..." He noticed they were both giving him a weird look. "It doesn't matter. You can look it up on the net."

They placed the IonoEngine in a clear space. "We all hold on to this," said Dev, motioning to the circular ring around the engine that had attached it to the craft, and which now provided a convenient handhold.

Next he pulled batteries no bigger than a mobile phone from the craft, and connected them to wires, which he yanked out of the cockpit dashboard.

He closed his eyes and ran his hand around the engine as if searching for something. "That's all green and smooth," he said cryptically. When he opened his eyes he saw Lot staring at him.

"You're being weird again," she warned.

"I'm just trying to see how this works."

"You do know that makes you sound weirder?"

Dev didn't have time to explain. He slipped a battery into Lot's pocket and attached the wires to a port in the ring. He repeated the process for Mason and himself, although he didn't plug his own battery in.

"We'll have enough juice to gently lift us up," said Dev, "and we'll keep going up like a helium balloon. We hang on and swing our bodies in the direction we want to move and the engine will drift that way. Got it?"

The other two nodded reluctantly; Mason somewhat more reluctantly than Lot. "If this place has so many gadgets, where are the rocket packs?" he huffed.

"In a more secure zone," said Dev. "You know in a movie when the hero gets all the cool gadgets at the beginning, then it just so happens that every situation he comes to is perfectly suited for the tech he has?" Mason nodded. "Well, this is *nothing* like that. We have to improvise with what we've got – so let's do it."

Standing equal distances apart, they knelt and held on to the IonoEngine's mounting ring. Dev plugged his battery into the port. "Here we go!"

There was a faint sizzle of air, and the hairs on his arm rose as the current surged through the engine.

Then it began to rise. Their movements were enough to gently steer the ring towards the edge of the unit before they ascended towards the shelf above.

"*Oh god, oh god, oh god...*" Mason muttered as his feet slid off the edge of the shelf.

Dev felt the firm ledge under his feet disappear, but he didn't look down. He kept his gaze on Lot, who was grinning like an idiot.

"This is brilliant!" she shrieked, before lowering her voice in case they were overheard. "I love it!"

Clear of the shelf, the engine righted itself and they rose silently upwards. Their speed was no more than walking pace, and Dev could feel his arms beginning to ache. He mentally kicked himself for not lashing his belt around the ring to secure him. If his arms gave up now, he would plunge to his death. Maybe he should have mentioned that to Lot and Mason too. He kept his eyes on their destination above, trying to ignore the drop below.

Still they rose. The gentle movement and lack of noise made the journey feel safe, and Dev could almost ignore the deadly drop. Out of the corner of his eye he saw they had not only cleared the elevator pit but the shelving stacks in the rest of the Inventory too. With a tremor of panic he calculated that they were at least eight storeys up. . .

And rising.

Watching the catwalk draw nearer was a painfully slow experience, and ignoring the aching in his arms was becoming increasingly difficult.

The catwalk was almost in arm's reach. Twenty more seconds and they would be there.

Then a soft bleep caught their attention. They all looked around, wondering where the sound was coming from.

"Mase, you're bleeping," said Lot, who had traced the noise to Mason's pocket. "There's a light flashing in your pocket . . . it's the battery."

"Oh no. . ." Dev felt his arms go weak as he realized what was happening. "It's a battery warning. They've been in storage for decades ... we should have charged them!"

Lot stared at Dev. "Are you telling me..." She trailed off as the IonoEngine began to slow.

Dev made the mistake of looking down. He could see his trainers dangling in the air – and then *far* below his feet were canyons of shelving units that looked like the network of streets at the bottom of a high-rise metropolis.

He suddenly felt weak. His fingers began to slip, and it felt as if gravity was clawing at him – determined to pluck them from the sky.

At that moment the IonoEngine stopped its ascent. They hovered in the air, just out of reach of the catwalk and safety.

ENGINE FAILURE

Frantically Dev grabbed at the catwalk rail. It was tantalizingly out of reach. His other arm was trembling with the effort of holding on to the IonoEngine's mounting ring. "Try swinging," he said, struggling to control the panic in his voice.

All three of them flung out their legs in an attempt to build momentum. Mason was the heaviest, and as his body lurched on the far side of the ring, the engine began to drift in the opposite direction from the catwalk.

"STOP!" yelled Dev.

Mason stopped wriggling and the engine righted

itself into a stationary hover. Dev strained for the catwalk again – but it was no good.

BEEP.

Now his battery joined the doom-laden choir.

"As the power goes, we'll just drift down, right? Like a feather?" Lot asked with as much optimism as she could muster.

Dev admired her ability to remain so upbeat when they were close to certain death. "No. We'll drop like a stone," he replied. "That's one of the safety issues with IonoCraft."

"Guaranteed death?" said Mason. "That's one heck of a safety issue. Well, mate, thanks for getting us killed."

"I've never been your 'mate'," growled Dev as his free hand grabbed the engine's ring to take the strain off his other aching arm. What should he do now? His uncle had taught him to see problems from different angles. *Take a step back and see the whole picture,* Charles Parker often said. While dangling above the ground was a physical handicap, Dev took a mental step back and tried to expel the fear that was clouding his judgement.

The walkway was level with them and just out of reach. He needed to get on top of the problem. Literally.

With a grunt he heaved himself up on to the engine

ring. Dev had never been very good at chin-ups, but now, his adrenaline flowing, he found the movement easy. One moment he had been terrified of heights. The next, his focus was entirely on the problem and its solution, and everything else was forgotten. He wondered if this was another side effect of his *special condition.*

The engine wobbled as he hoisted acrobatically himself up. The ring was about the diameter of a hula hoop and only a few centimetres wide – but it was enough for him to swing his foot on to.

"What are you doing?" said Lot, fear quaking her voice.

Dev didn't answer. He knew he needed all his concentration on the task in hand; it was the only thing that was making him forget his fear of heights. One crisis at a time, he reminded himself.

He swung his second foot on to the ring and slowly stood up, arms stretched out either side to keep his balance. He was now standing on top of the engine, balanced like a tightrope walker on the thin mounting ring. He moved with ease, as if he'd done crazy things like this all his life. He was careful not to stand on the wiring within the engine itself – not only was it fragile enough to break at the slightest pressure, but it also had thousands of volts coursing through it. Dev knew it would fry him in an instant.

"Hurry!" warned Lot as the engine trembled.

Dev braced himself – then leapt for the catwalk.

His stomach slammed into the handrail, and he folded around it, holding on tightly as his feet failed to find grip on the catwalk and slipped off – pulling him down.

His arms ached as he tightened his grip on the handrail to stop his fall. With a grunt of effort, he hauled himself on to the relative safety of the narrow catwalk.

He hadn't noticed that the wire running from the battery in his pocket to the engine had pulled taut. The plug snapped out of the port on the mounting ring – disconnecting him from the engine.

The IonoEngine shuddered from the sudden loss of power – and Lot and Mason screamed. Luckily, without Dev's weight, they remained hovering in place.

"I'm going to pull you across!" Dev shouted across. "Catch!"

He threw his battery towards Lot, keeping hold of the other end. With both her hands holding on to the ring for dear life, she made no attempt to catch it – and it struck her left cheek.

"OW!" she shrieked.

"I said catch it!" Dev reeled the wire in – then threw it out again. This time Mason lunged for it. "Don't let go!"

Dev pulled the wire. With their weight suspended by the IonoEngine, it was easy to draw them closer. Little by little they moved towards the catwalk.

"It's working!" cried Lot.

The warning tone from Mason's battery suddenly stopped, and the IonoEngine lurched as it lost power. Lot and Mason didn't need to be told what to do – they both swung for the catwalk—

Just as the engine dropped.

Mason landed hard against the catwalk as Dev had done – and for a moment it looked as if he would rebound off it. Dev grabbed his arm and pulled him to safety. The battery in Mason's pocket was yanked out as the power line snapped.

Lot landed gracefully on the outer edge of the catwalk. She had one leg over the rail, just as her battery lost power too.

"That was too close!" she gasped.

Only Dev saw that she was still in danger. He raced towards her as the IonoEngine plummeted towards the ground. Lot's battery wire had coiled around her leg as she jumped. The battery was wedged in a pocket of her combat trousers; the other end was jammed into the engine's mounting ring port.

The cable snapped tight from the weight of the falling engine and, twisted around Lot's leg, dragged her suddenly back over the edge.

Lot screamed. Then she felt Dev's arms around her, stopping her fall. The sudden yank on the cable snapped the wire free from the mounting ring – and the engine plunged to the ground.

Lot clung to Dev, breathing hard. He could feel her trembling. "It's OK," he said. "You're safe."

Through the mesh floor of the catwalk, they watched the engine strike the edge of a shelving unit with an almighty bang. It shattered into pieces that rained down across the aisle far below.

Lot slowly pulled away from Dev. She refused to meet his gaze. "That was fun," she said with forced cheerfulness.

They took in their new surroundings at ceiling level. The catwalk stretched across the warehouse in both directions, suspended from the roof by metal poles that barely looked capable of supporting their weight. Occasionally there were crossroads where other walkways joined it, forming a larger grid. They could see the walls of the warehouse from here, while the forest of shelves prevented them from seeing much in the aisles below. Metal conduits ran just above their heads, housing cables, air-conditioning pipes and the powerful spotlights that illuminated the space below.

Then Dev spotted what they were looking for. A relay box bolted on to a mass of cables.

"This is a relay for the computer system," he said as he unclipped a panel, revealing the complex circuitry behind it. The Inventory's wireless network had been compromised, and there was no way he could risk plugging directly into the system with his watch, but Dev had one last trick up his sleeve.

"SNFC – super near field communication," he said to the two uncomprehending faces peering over his shoulder. "Like the chips in credit cards that allow you to pay for things just by waving it in front of the reader. Only way more advanced."

Mason laughed. "You are such a nerd."

"Yeah, the nerd who just saved your life!" growled

Dev. "You shouldn't be here, remember?! You shouldn't have seen any of this!"

He rounded on Mason, shoving his hand so hard into Mason's chest that he took an involuntary step back – straight into the handrail – causing the whole catwalk to sway.

"Dev, don't. . ." said Lot.

Dev was too angry to listen. "I don't know why you're even with us. I should have left you behind for those thugs to deal with." Dev didn't know where his anger was coming from, but it felt good to unleash his feelings. He prodded Mason in the chest again. "You're just dead weight."

Mason went pale, glancing over the edge of the catwalk at the drop below.

Dev felt Lot's hand on his arm. "Easy, Dev. Like it or not, we're all in this together right now. Mase isn't one of *them*."

"How do you know that? Nobody has ever broken into the Inventory before. Not until today!" Dev studied her. "And you're always backing him up. Typical." His resentment towards Mason was overflowing on to her now. "Looks like I've got to babysit you both, then."

He was seething with anger. All his life he had been

the geeky kid ignored by cool, popular kids like Lot and Mason, yet now they were looking to him for help? It was so unfair.

He pushed past Lot and turned his attention to the access port. He lifted his watch so it was a millimetre from a small sensor. Accessing the hacker app he had spent last summer creating, he soon bypassed the hijacked security and accessed his Trojan program. He hoped that, virtually hidden there, the attackers would be unable to stop him.

Data flowed over his watch's holographic display. He moved his free hand and a virtual keyboard appeared mid-air. He rapidly typed a series of codes. The scrolling data paused, then was replaced by a flashing old-school cursor.

"All right! We're in." He beamed. "They haven't managed to break into my Trojan." He frowned. "But there's something else in here too. . ."

A three-dimensional hologram of Eema's emoji projected from his watch and floated in front of his face. Rather than the usual smug smile, this face looked concerned and frightened.

"Devon, thank goodness you're OK!" said Eema urgently. "I have been unable to see you on my systems."

"That's because I cloaked us from the security system," Dev replied. "Wait a second, how do I know you are ... *you*? I thought the intruders had disabled you."

"Almost," said Eema. "They deleted my main quantum drives. If I hadn't managed to download my artificial intelligence files into your Trojan, then they would have found me and deleted me."

"So it looks like I saved you too." He threw a glance at Lot and Mason.

The emoji looked at him curiously. "How you managed to place a Trojan in *my* software..." Eema shook her head indignantly. "It's disgusting. Lucky for us both that I found it. However, my ability to help you has been compromised. I can't access the husks while the main security is jammed, and only your uncle can deactivate that. So if you see a security robot then *they* must be controlling it. You must find the Iron Fist and then leave the Inventory immediately."

Dev paused. The intruders had compromised Eema. How did he know he could trust the computer? Who was to say that Eema wasn't under their control already?

"Not just yet, Eema. I want to know where my uncle is."

"Charles Parker is unharmed, but held captive. They are using him as a knowledge resource to override security protocols. However, that won't work. Once the Inventory is locked down, even I can't control all the security."

"Who are they?"

"As far as I am able to discern, they are a group of Double Helix mercenaries."

Dev looked at Lot and Mason to see if the name meant anything to them. They shook their heads. "Who are Double Helix?"

"You are not authorized to know that."

Dev groaned. "Eema, come on! I need to know who is after us!"

"From my observations, this particular unit is governed by the Collector." Eema's emoji was replaced by a picture of the fiend. "He is known as a high-level operative within Shadow Helix."

"How does the Collector know about this place? The weapons they have . . . they look like they belong in here."

"You are not authorized to know that."

Dev was growing angry. "They mentioned something called Iron Fist. What is it?"

"You are not authorized to know that." This time it was Mason's voice mimicking Eema. Dev shot him a scathing look.

The image of the Collector was replaced by a gauntlet that appeared to be made from a blue metal. Rather than the sleek designs Dev was accustomed to from comic books, this had wires, tubes and coils hanging from it, a sure sign it was an experimental piece of technology rather than the finished product.

Eema spoke as Dev rotated the image. "This is all I found on the Inventory archive. The Iron Fist relic is as yet unclassified. It was discovered in the Scrap Chamber last year, and current research points to the design belonging to Nikola Tesla."

"Wow!" said Dev.

"Tesla? Like the car?" asked Lot.

Dev shook his head. "No. Elon Musk invented those." He saw Mason was about to ask who *he* was, so pressed quickly on. "Nikola Tesla was one of the world's greatest inventors. He was from Serbia, but lived in America. He specialized in researching electricity and he created some amazing things. But, as usual, the world wasn't ready for him." He shook his head sadly. "He died penniless. And in his final years his best friend was a pigeon. He even thought aliens were projecting plans into his brain."

Mason tapped his head. "Weirdo. I guess that's why you like him. That and the fact he invented a whole bunch of useless rubbish."

"You're right," said Dev. "Of course he also invented the AC electricity we all use, the fluorescent light bulb, the radio—"

"Marconi invented the radio," said Lot, proud she knew a fact.

Dev shook his head. "Nope. Look it up. Tesla also invented the remote control – oh, and the electric motor. Just like in the cars." Dev looked pointedly at Mason. "So, yeah. What a *loser.*"

He took a deep breath and turned back to Eema, whose emoji had reappeared. "And what does the Iron Fist do?"

"I don't know," Eema replied. "But evidently the Collector is desperate to obtain it. There have been a number of reported deaths that have been linked to researchers on Project Iron Fist. Studying the police files, I have calculated an eighty-six per cent likelihood that the Collector is behind them. The Iron Fist is being held in the Red Zone for further analysis."

"That's right in the heart of the Inventory," Dev said. "They can't get in there."

Eema paused before speaking again. Dev wasn't sure if it was for effect or if even quantum computers struggled to be tactful. "I'm afraid the probability that they will break into the Red Zone is high. They will use Charles Parker. Knowing how the Collector works, your uncle's life will be at stake."

"So I need to rescue my uncle from them?"

"No. You need to get Iron Fist before they do. The Iron Fist relic has the potential for catastrophic damage. Charles Parker's life is irrelevant compared with ensuring the relic does not fall into the wrong hands."

Dev's stomach knotted. He was used to Eema's callous comments, but to be told that their lives were a pale second to some odd invention hidden in the Inventory, *that* was sickening.

Lot stepped forward so Eema could see her. "Are you telling us we can't leave?"

The emoji spun around to face her. "Not without the Iron Fist. If the Collector wants it, then it is imperative he doesn't get it. The only way is forward."

Mason spoke up. "I don't want to be trapped in the middle of this place."

Eema glanced at him. "You won't be. In the Red Zone there is a way out. A one-way teleport system used for evacuation."

"A teleporter?" It was the first time Dev had heard about that. "But, Eema, how can we possibly get ahead of them? If a group of heavily armed mercenaries is going to struggle to get into the further zones, then we don't stand a chance!"

"I believe you do, Devon. All the time you have spent here with your uncle. With your knowledge... Devon, this is what you were bred for."

"I'm not a dog!" he laughed. He knew he should be feeling angry, but he actually enjoyed the rare praise. Maybe he *could* actually achieve something worthwhile.

Dev snapped his fingers. "The Vacuum-Pods may have been deactivated, but the tunnel system is still in one piece, right?"

"Yes."

"And they still connect the zones together?"

"Some of them at least. That is an excellent idea. I can pressurize the system now," Eema replied. "When you reach the portal to the Red Zone I will not be able to help you, not while I am hidden within the Trojan. You must get through yourself."

"How do I do that?"

Lot suddenly spoke up. "Dev! Somebody's coming!"

Dev didn't look away from Eema's emoji face as she continued. "There are several possible defence mechanisms that will be activated, I can't tell you which. What I can tell you is that the way ahead follows the rule of six."

Dev shook his head. "Rule of six? What does that mean?"

"Dev!" hissed Lot. "We have to go!"

They peered down. Kwolek was leading a small knot of goons in the aisle below. They watched as one of the mercenaries found fragments of the broken IonoEngine and raised the alarm. Now the others rushed to join him.

Dev remembered the question that had been burning in his brain. His voice dropped into a whisper. "Eema, how did they break into the Inventory in the first place? I thought it was supposed to be impossible to bypass security."

"It is," Eema replied coolly. "They must have had help from somebody on the *inside*."

Dev's mouth went dry. So there really was a traitor in his midst. His eyes darted to Mason – then back to the figures below.

Kwolek was looking up and pointing straight at them. They had been spotted.

This was confirmed moments later when the air shimmered and a sonic blast destroyed one of the poles supporting the catwalk above their heads.

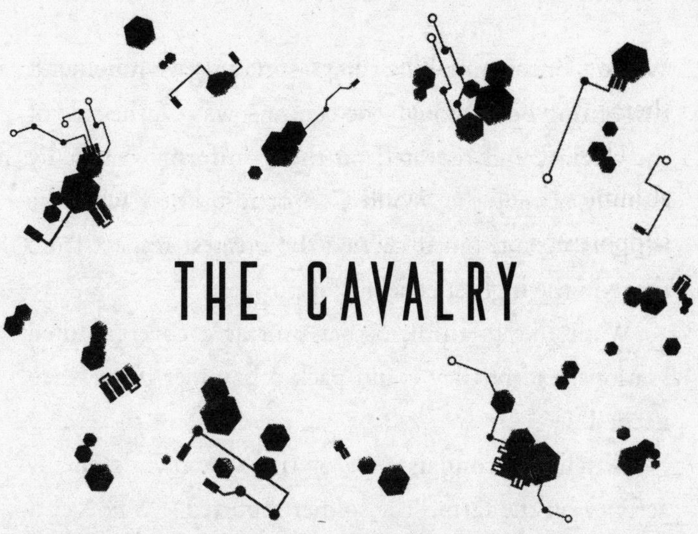

THE CAVALRY

Heavy combat boots clanked rhythmically as a group of special forces soldiers ran up the ramp of the three huge Chinook helicopters. Already the engines were spooling up, the spinning rotors blasting a heavy breeze on the troops below.

They were watched by Sergeant Wade. Nobody would have seen it through her cool professionalism, but ever since Eema had triggered the Inventory's intruder alert, Wade had felt uneasy at the sheer scale of the assault.

A Chinese solider ran up to her and saluted smartly. These were not soldiers from one single country; they came from the elite ranks of every member state of the

World Consortium. Their logo – an omega symbol with a lightning bolt through the centre – was on the side of the aircraft and repeated on their uniforms. Virtually nobody outside the World Consortium knew what the insignia meant, but it carried the greatest respect from those in the highest echelons of power.

Wade like to think of her unit as a covert United Nations, except they could pack a hammer blow when needed.

"Satellite reconnaissance of the area reveals enemy activity on the farm," the soldier reported. "Whoever it is, it looks as if they're expecting us."

Wade thanked the soldier and turned her attention back to the aircraft as the heavy weaponry was loaded. The arms being piled into the helicopters were nothing as primitive as guns. Wade's team had technology developed from the very best the Inventory had to offer. It was *beyond* next-generation.

With everybody and everything loaded, she jogged towards the lead Chinook and up the ramp. It began to close, the machine lifting from the runway, before she was even midway up.

Sergeant Wade wasn't worried about the fight to come. She was more concerned about what was happening in the Inventory at that very moment. She was one of only six people who knew the truth of what was down there. And right now she knew everything hinged on the shoulders of one boy. . .

DOWN THE TUBE

Dev, Lot and Mason fell on their backs as the catwalk shuddered violently beneath them.

"They're going to shoot us down!" screamed Mason.

Dev hated that Mason was always pointing out the obvious. As another sonic pulse punctured a perfectly circular hole through the metal grating between his legs, Dev leapt to his feet, hauling Lot upright.

"Go! Go!" he said, starting to run. "They can't get up here."

Below them, Kwolek and her team ran along the aisle, easily matching their progress.

Dev reached a crossroads and veered right. Mason was

still lagging behind as another volley of shots destroyed the catwalk behind them. They watched in horror as the damaged walkway peeled away from the ceiling and cascaded down. The one advantage: the falling walkway forced the soldiers to scatter. One mercenary had nowhere to run as the walkway dropped straight on to him.

Up above, the combined weight of Dev, Lot and Mason caused the remaining catwalk to sag and wobble, like a ruler hanging over the edge of a desk. More supporting spars snapped from the roof and the severed end of the catwalk began to curve downwards. Mason lost his footing first – then slid into Dev and Lot. All three tumbled down the incline towards the drop.

Lot's fingers clung to the mesh floor and she howled in pain as Dev bumped into her, stomping on her fingers. Dev grabbed the twisted handrail, finally stopping his fall.

Mason wasn't so lucky. He was on his back and sliding too fast. His legs were already over the edge...

He was suddenly pulled to a halt, the collar of his jacket choking him as it pulled tight. Lot had managed to reach out with one hand and snag his collar, stopping his descent – but supporting herself with one hand was already weakening her grip.

"Dev! Help me!"

Dev began a controlled descent towards Mason. He secured one foot against a section of the rail to brace himself – then reached down. The yawning drop beneath them made his head spin.

"Take my hand!"

Mason moved with agonizing slowness. He was staring at Kwolek below, her sonic weapon trained upon them. One shot and they would all die.

"Mason! Take my hand or you'll fall!" Dev yelled, straining forward.

Lot groaned in pain, and her fingers supporting Mason began to tremble. "Mase, I can't hold on much longer."

Mason snatched Dev's hand. Dev grunted as he heaved him up. "Why . . . are you so . . . heavy?" he grunted.

Mason twisted around to grasp hold of the handrail. His grip on Dev slipped and his fingers hooked on to Dev's watch. Dev howled as the watch strap dug into his skin. Mason's weight was too great – and the strap snapped.

Mason fell, the watch clutched in his hand.

With a scream, Mason swung out, letting go of

the watch to grab the handrail and stop his fall. Dev watched in horror as his watch, their lifeline – the only communication he had with Eema – plummeted to the floor.

Free to move again, Lot helped Mason to scramble back up on to the sagging walkway, and the two of them clambered to the secure and level section.

"Dev, come on!" Lot urged.

Dev tore his gaze away from his watch and joined them just as Kwolek fired again, blasting the hanging walkway to pieces. Now he ran for all he was worth and didn't look back. Only the clatter of their footsteps assured him that Lot and Mason were close behind.

"We're sitting ducks up here," Mason panted as Dev took a left at another junction.

But they also had the head start they needed. Below, the intruders couldn't move as freely, forced to change directions every time the shelving units ran to an end.

Dev led Lot and Mason to a large tube, about the diameter of a van, that ran along the ceiling. One end stretched vertically up from the floor, before curving where it met the ceiling. The other end ran straight through a distant wall.

Dev ran his fingers across the surface, his eyes closed.

Where his fingers stopped, he pressed the surface. A hidden access panel slid open with a gentle hiss. It was just big enough for them to crawl through.

"Inside, quickly."

Lot peered into the dark space beyond. "How did you find this, Dev? We couldn't see this from the outside."

"I told you. I have gift for this kind of thing. Now, come on. . ." He indicated into the tube.

Mason entered first, using his mobile phone to illuminate the dark interior. Lot threw a questioning glance at Dev, then followed.

Dev peered below to check that Kwolek hadn't spotted them, but she and her team were nowhere to be seen. Taking a deep breath, he entered the dark tube and sealed it behind them.

A STEP AHEAD

Lee gazed at the door leading to the Blue Zone. It remained resolutely closed. He would rather have stayed in the command bunker, but so far his team had failed. He had no wish to report back to the Collector that they had been unable to open a door.

He glanced at Charles Parker. "Well, Professor Parker, if you could just open it up, then you will save us a lot of effort."

"You know I can't do that."

Lee sighed and waved his hand to one of his men. "OK, we'll stick to Plan A and blow this thing wide open."

The muscular man cracked his knuckles and climbed on board the tank that they had taken from a display. It was unusual in that it had no tracks. The driver's head poked from the hatch at the front and the machine rumbled to life, rising on a cushion of sparks and emitting a loud crackling noise that drowned out any conversation. Once it was a metre off the ground the noise abated and the HoverTank silently drifted forward.

"All right!" Lee yelled. "Batter up!"

The tank's barrel swivelled around to face the door. The engine began to hum and lights strobed down the barrel as it built up a charge.

Charles Parker shook his head. "You plan to shoot your way through the door? I'm afraid that won't work."

Lee wagged a finger. "Do you know why the HoverTank never made it to front-line combat? Aside from the awful start-up noise, of course. The energy weapon was made from a standard terawatt laser. Useless. My guys have replaced it with a zero-point energy cannon from one of your other little relics back there."

Charles Parker looked uncomfortable. "The zero-point cannon was never fully tested. It could collapse every particle in the door, thus creating a small black hole. . ."

"Exactly! And that would collapse the door on itself."

"Or escalate out of control and suck the entire Inventory down to the size of a pinhead!"

A shadow of doubt crossed Lee's face. "That would kill us all."

"Possibly."

The sliver of hope Charles had been clinging to was suddenly extinguished when Lee burst into laughter.

"Oh, Prof. You really think that hadn't occurred to us?" Lee pointed at him. "The look on your face was classic. You almost thought I'd turn around and quit, didn't you? Well, newsflash, that is not going to happen." He turned to the tank driver. "Fire away!"

The tank suddenly emitted a brilliant light. Charles Parker looked away, shielding his eyes as a tongue of energy rolled lazily from the barrel and struck the centre of the door.

With a terrible crunching sound of tortured metal, the door folded in on itself, shrinking so fast that a hurricane force drew them towards it. Charles Parker's ears popped and he was dragged closer to the door, his leather-soled shoes skidding across the smooth floor.

In seconds the storm abated. Charles looked up and was astonished to see the door was no longer there. Neither was a ragged chunk of wall around it.

A gaping portal now led into the Blue Zone.

The driver killed the tank's engine and the machine dropped to the floor with a resounding clang.

Lee strode forward into the next zone. "It seems your Inventory is open for business after all."

Suddenly a voice came over his headset. Lee stopped in his tracks and listened with concern.

"All units, we have visitors outside. And Kwolek has news about the kids."

Turning away from the newly opened portal, Lee hurried back towards the bunker.

THE TUNNEL

The tunnel was smooth and featureless. The light from Lot's and Mason's phones failed to reveal anything ahead. It was as if they were walking into a black hole; and it felt as if they had been walking for miles, which Dev thought was probably close to the truth.

"Are you certain they won't find us in here?" asked Lot. "It's not as if there is anywhere to hide."

"Relax, they won't look in here," said Dev confidently. "Nobody would think of looking in here. This is the old Vacuum-Pod system. Have you ever seen those air suction tubes they used to use in banks in old films?"

Mason laughed. "Yeah. They'd pop canisters full of cash inside and they'd be sucked into the vault."

"Exactly. It's that except on a bigger scale. Without air there is no resistance, so the pods could shoot through the tunnels faster than a train. You might have noticed the suction has been deactivated or we would have been there already."

Lot suddenly stopped and shone her light behind them. "I thought I heard something."

They all strained to listen, but couldn't hear anything.

"Don't worry," Dev assured her, "the Vacuum-Pods can't operate if there's air in here. Besides, it hasn't been used for years. My uncle shut it all down when the security was improved."

They continued walking in silence. Dev's mind was churning through what Eema had said about the Collector needing help from somebody on the inside. That confirmed his suspicion: it was no coincidence that Lot and Mason had turned up on the farm at the very same time as the attack. Either of them could be the mole. His natural suspicions fell on Mason, especially now that Mason had caused him to lose his watch, their only contact with Eema, leaving them blind as they delved deeper into the Inventory. But could he really trust Lot either? She hadn't spoken to him for years, then suddenly. . .

Ahead, the tunnel began to sharply curve downwards. Steps had been moulded into the floor, presumably to allow people to service the tunnel. They descended cautiously, their phones illuminating the utter darkness only a few metres ahead.

"Stop!" Dev said suddenly.

In the darkness he almost hadn't seen that there was no more tunnel ahead of them – instead it inclined sharply downwards. Dev had expected this. It meant they had crossed into the Blue Zone already and the almost-vertical drop would take them to the next Pod stop. He had hoped for a ladder or some other way down, but there was nothing.

"It's a dead end," Lot said. "Or it will be for us if we carry on."

Just then they became aware of a faint whirling noise behind them. They spun around to see a small disc-shaped drone hovering at the edge of the pool of illumination created by Mason's mobile. The light reflected off the dome of a small thumb-sized camera. Whoever was operating it had definitely seen them.

With a bellow, Mason lunged for the hovering object.

REVENGE

Lee recoiled from the screen as the oversized image of Mason filled it. They had a view straight into the boy's mouth before the picture cut to black.

Lee leaned back in his chair. "Looks like that kid owes you a drone."

He grinned at Kwolek, who was sitting the wrong way round on another chair as she watched the transmission. She shook her head, impressed. Her men had lost sight of Dev and his companions after they narrowly escaped being shot down on the walkway, but she had found the watch and returned to the control bunker with it. It hadn't taken Lee long to find

Eema's last command from the watch was to flood the Vacuum-Pod tubes with air. The twins had then accessed the tubes and flown a drone inside to see if the kids were really there.

"I have to ask," said Lee conversationally, "what kind of name is Kwolek? I mean, why choose *that* as a code name?"

"Why choose Lee?" she replied without taking her eyes off the screens. "I mean, Faraday, Edison, they're obvious. But Lee? It's kinda boring."

Lee shrugged as if it was obvious, but Kwolek clearly didn't get it. "Tim Berners-Lee?" She shook her head. "Give me strength," he muttered. "He only invented that little thing called *the Internet*. What did Kwolek invent? The rubber band?" He laughed at his own dumb joke.

Kwolek snorted with derision. "She was the genius who created the bulletproof vest. That saved my life on more than one occasion, let me tell you." She continued to stare at the blank screen. "What would happen if you turned the tubes back into a vacuum?"

"They'd suffocate and die. No need to do that. Inside there they're not going anywhere. They're no longer a problem for us. I need you to focus on the main task at hand."

Lee turned his attention to a radar screen that showed three World Consortium Chinooks bearing down on the farm.

"The cavalry is right on time. Impressive."

Kwolek didn't answer. Lee turned around, but she had left the bunker. He adjusted his headset and patched his communication link directly to the surface team. "OK, people, we have three incoming bogeys. Get ready."

Kwolek hurried back to the supply room, where the laptop was connected to the security system. While she was no expert black-hat hacker like Lee, she could navigate through the laptop and locate the controls to purge the air from the tube network, reverting it back to a vacuum.

No matter what Lee had said, she was certain the Collector wouldn't want any loose ends – and those annoying kids were definitely loose ends. Plus they had made a fool of her, which made them targets for her revenge.

She quickly found the controls for the vacuum tunnel system. It was an old interface with tick boxes and sliding controls that looked as if it had been designed last century. The click of a mouse was all that was needed to start the powerful pumps that would suck the air from the tubes in just over a minute.

Then she returned to Lee to watch the battle on the surface unfold.

AIR TIME

The way Mason held up the broken drone as a spoil of victory reminded Dev of a faithful hound retrieving a stick. He wondered how he could have suspected Mason was a traitor. An idiot and a bully, sure, but a traitor?

He glanced at Lot. She was smiling her infectious smile at Mason, and this too vaporized any notion in Dev's mind that she was working with the bad guys.

Then a dark thought struck him – maybe that was the perfect cover?

He felt a sudden breeze against his face. His immediate fear was that a Vacuum-Pod was hurtling towards them, but he knew that was impossible with air in the tunnel.

The breeze suddenly turned into a hurricane that threatened to roll them back down the tunnel. The wind stung his eyes and they began to water.

"What's going on?" Lot yelled above the increasing roar.

Dev knew exactly what was happening. "They're sucking out the air! They're turning the tube back into a vacuum!"

Dev knew that if they didn't do something fast they would suffocate. His first instinct was to run back the way they had come, but the access panel he had closed behind them was already too far away. That left one other option.

"We're going to have to jump!" he shouted.

"Are you crazy?" Mason screamed back.

"We jump – or we suffocate in less than a minute!"

With streaming eyes, they peered into the void below. The air blasted them in the face so hard that their jowls flapped like flags.

"It could work," said Lot with growing excitement. "The wind's strong enough. If we open our jackets, it should help slow our descent." Even in the dim light she could see Mason's dubious expression. "I did a tandem parachute jump with my dad once. We're not going to sail down like a feather, but it should be enough to act as an air brake."

Dev unzipped his jacket and gripped both sides, ready to open it like a wing the moment he took the plunge. "If we're going to do this, we're going to have to jump *now!*" He stood on the edge. The darkness beyond soothed him; not being able to see the perils below eased his vertigo. He was certain that if the tube was lit he would be quaking in his trainers.

"Mase, you have to do this," Lot urged.

Mason didn't move; he looked terrified.

"It's either this or we suffocate."

"Come on! Go now! NOW!" bellowed Dev, and he leapt head first into the darkness.

Lot followed immediately.

Dev's stomach lurched as it did when his uncle drove over a bridge too fast, except it didn't settle back again as he plummeted down the tube. He screamed with both fear and exhilaration. He spread his arms, opening his jacket. It immediately inflated as the air filled it, expanding the material, and he felt himself slow a little.

Lot shot past him with a scream. She was still

clutching her mobile phone as a light and he could see the wall zipping past them in a blur. She opened her jacket moments later and her speed reduced to match Dev's.

Seconds later Mason tumbled past, spinning head over heels. He tried to open his jacket but the fabric tore from his hand and left him free-falling. The illumination from his phone spun around and around, marking his trajectory. The wind slowed his descent a little, but Dev was certain it wouldn't be enough.

Just as sharply as it had started, the ferocious wind ceased, and Dev and Lot found themselves plummeting straight down, even faster now that there was almost zero air friction.

The side of the tube raced towards them, and Dev remembered that the tubes were not completely vertical; they arced steadily near the bottom to allow the Vacuum-Pods to level out at the ground floor.

They landed on the slope, transitioning from a free fall to riding a huge death slide. They were sliding so fast they could feel the friction heat through their clothes. If any bare skin touched the tube, it would be flayed clean off.

The tube's arc increased so dramatically that they

were horizontal before they knew it and rolled along the floor for several metres before sliding to a stop. The two mobile phones had escaped Lot's and Mason's clutches and skittered on a little further, still providing just enough illumination.

Dev laughed with relief – but no sound came out. With horror, he realized they were now in a vacuum. There was no air to carry sound.

There was no air to breathe.

But breathing wasn't their biggest problem. Dev knew what happened to astronauts if their pressurized suits tore in the vacuum of space.

They exploded.

His eyes felt strange, as if a pressure was building from behind. His skin began to prickle as, without any air pressure against him, the blood vessels across his body began to expand.

There wasn't a moment to lose.

Dev ran for the nearest mobile phone. He needed some light to open the door once he found it. His whole body felt as if needles were stabbing him, and his legs trembled as he stooped to pick up the phone.

He turned around and almost bumped into Lot. He screamed – but no sound came out. Lot's face was beginning to swell – her eyes bulging from their sockets.

Judging by her reaction, he must have looked equally dreadful. He pushed past her and ran towards where the door should be. In order to maintain a vacuum, the doors had to close with precision, so were almost invisible from either side of the tunnel.

Dev tried to close his eyes and focus, but his eyelids were unable to cover his swelling eyeballs. He ran his hands across the wall and saw a swirling cloud of colours. He hoped it was from his gift rather than his brain playing tricks due to lack of oxygen.

His peculiar sixth sense told him he was touching the door. He held up the phone and, in the pale light, he could just make out the mechanism that automatically opened the door when a pod arrived. It was a simple mechanical switch the Vacuum-Pod turned when it ran over it at speed. Dev frantically kicked it – but he lacked the strength to move it. It hadn't been used for so long it had seized in position.

Just to the side was an access panel with a clear glass window showing the emergency-open button behind it. All he had to do was break the glass and push it.

Dev mustered his strength and punched the glass. He was so weak he delivered it with all the force of a pensioner. Each strike was weaker than the last as his strength ebbed.

His mind was fogging. He needed to focus on the problem. He shone the phone around for something to break the glass with. There was nothing.

Except the phone.

Dev put all his weight behind the phone and used its corner to strike the glass. The emergency glass fractured just enough for him to worm a finger inside.

With fading vision he pushed the emergency release button.

Nothing happened.

He pressed it again and again.

Still the door didn't open.

Now his lungs burned and he felt light-headed due to the lack of oxygen. He was vaguely aware of Mason slumping to the floor, but tried to ignore him. Dev placed his finger, swollen and red as the blood vessels inside had expanded, and concentrated on the circuits beyond the switch. Components that had started to corrode with age . . . but there was still *some* spark left in them.

The silence was suddenly punctured by a roar as the door unlocked and was violently jolted inwards from the air pressure outside. It thudded against a groove around the doorway and Lot was able to slide it open. Air rapidly flooded inside the tunnel with similar hurricane force as before. Their eyes stung and they clung to the wall to prevent themselves from being blown away.

In seconds the air pressure equalized, popping their ears once more, and they staggered from the tube, dropping to their knees as they gulped the air.

Dev marvelled just how thick the air tasted in his mouth; it was as if he were breathing water. Still slumped in the tunnel, Mason stirred as he sucked in huge lungfuls of air. It took a few minutes for everything to feel normal. Only then did they risk looking at one another. Their swollen faces had settled back down, although their eyes were bloodshot. Their skin was red, as if they had terrible sunburns.

Lot began to giggle.

Mason crawled from the tunnel to join them. "What's so funny?"

"That was the *worst* feeling I have ever experienced," she said between fits of giggles. The other two broke into laughter, drunk on oxygen.

It took another minute or so before they could catch their breath and wipe the tears from their eyes, by which time the redness of their faces had dulled away.

"Remind me again why we're doing this?" said Mason, rubbing his temples. "Instead of just hiding and letting somebody else deal with the problem."

"What if they get to the Iron Fist before help arrives?" said Lot.

"What if no help's coming?" Dev sombrely added. He immediately regretted saying it. "Come on. The only way is forward."

They stood up on shaking legs and looked around the new warehouse they had entered.

Dev knew he must have been here before but he didn't recognize any of it. He guessed the new layout that greeted them was due to the security lockdown, but he had no idea how they were going to get through it.

Lot shook her head in wonder. "At least I know why it's called the *Blue Zone*."

BATTLE FOR THE FARM

Sergeant Wade gripped the hanging strap as the Chinook banked sharply. The strap was all that kept her inside the aircraft now that the tail ramp was down. The ground rolled past four hundred metres below – and the missile they were avoiding roared past on a column of flame and smoke.

"Alpha team – deploy now!" she bellowed.

The eight soldiers with her didn't hesitate. They ran full speed along the ramp and leapt from the helicopter. Once they were clear, Wade readied herself to jump, pausing only to watch as one of her Chinooks was struck by another missile from below, the aircraft's fuselage cracking in two. With a rotor apiece, the two halves spun in different directions as they plummeted to the fields below. She hoped that the troopers inside had managed to evacuate.

With no time for regret, Wade dived head first out of the aircraft.

The ground raced up to greet her, but she controlled her descent by extending her legs and arms, fully opening the wingsuit she wore. It was a more sophisticated version of the method that Dev, Lot and Mason had attempted far underground. The fabric wings that extended between her arms, legs and body had been precision engineered.

The World Consortium team descended like hawks, nimbly banking between strands of laser fire from below. Wade was forced to barrel roll to avoid another missile and her whole body shook violently as she flew through the searing contrail.

Recovering quickly, Wade landed gracefully within the farm. She joined the rest of her team as they took cover behind one of the few barns still standing.

Securing the farm was going to be more difficult than she had anticipated. The enemy were armed with a hoard of exotic weaponry: de-atomizer lasers,

X-ray grenades and smart bullets. Items that should be prohibited and locked in the Inventory, but had somehow bypassed being confiscated.

Wade couldn't help but wonder what was going on underground. She glanced at her troops. None of them suspected that there was somebody below that she deeply cared for. She hoped they would escape unscathed.

THE BLUE ZONE

"Is it always like this?" asked Mason, rubbing the life back into his cheeks, still numb from the vacuum ordeal.

Almost the entire warehouse ahead of them was flooded, save the elevated section they stood on and another, three hundred metres away, from which a pier stretched out across the mirror-calm water, ending in steps that descended beneath the surface.

"I've never seen it like this before," said Dev thoughtfully. "It must be a security feature. Most of this storage area is a dry dock for ships, subs, that kind of thing. But the whole area must have been lowered and flooded to stop people getting into the Red Zone."

"So how do we get there?"

Dev pointed towards a far-off featureless wall and lowered his hand below the water line. "The door is around there." Neither Mason nor Lot responded. "Or we could go back through the tube system," he added, hoping they didn't think that was a good idea.

There was a duet of protest. Nobody wanted to experience the horrors of the vacuum tube again.

Ever.

Lot peered into the water, cupping her hands either side of her eyes to shield them from the lights above. "How deep do you think it is?"

"About two or three storeys," said Dev.

Mason scowled. "This is ridiculous! All I see is that you're dragging us deeper and deeper into some dangerously stupid scrapyard! Those people back there were shooting at us. Shooting! Then you nearly kill us with your crazy escape plan –" he pointed at the tube "– and now you expect us to drown? This has nothing to do with me! This is your mess!" In frustration he kicked the wall behind him.

Dev wanted to shout back, to unleash the frustration he felt inside, but he knew it would serve no purpose. To his surprise his voice came out low and even. "Fine.

Stay here. I don't care. I never invited you here anyway. You can sit down and wait for the angry soldiers with the energy weapons to turn up." He glanced at Lot as he added, "Both of you."

Mason looked away. The idea of waiting to be captured didn't appeal to him either.

Dev's gaze bored into Mason. "You know, I keep on thinking that it was all very convenient that you were hanging around the farm just as they turn up."

Mason held up his hand, indicating that he had said all he had to say on the matter.

Dev was struck by a detail he had overlooked and his thoughts came tumbling out. "It's odd. Eema's security systems are so sensitive that they picked up on Lot climbing over the gate. In the past they have stopped dozens of intruders who knew the security systems were there. But you ... you didn't know any of that and yet you managed to walk straight into a restricted barn without Eema detecting you." He looked levelly at Mason. "I'm really interested in how you achieved that, Mason."

Mason looked away, his cheeks flushing with guilt.

Lot's eye narrowed as she studied his face. In the rush of events it hadn't occurred to her that Mason's appearance had been suspicious. "Why were you really there, Mase?" she asked. She didn't want to believe he had anything to do with the attack, but the way he avoided looking at her fuelled her suspicions.

When Mason finally spoke up, his words were heavy. "Some guy . . . he offered me fifty quid if I just came here and hung around with you."

Dev moved to a panel in the wall, marked with a small emergency triangle. "What guy?"

Mason shook his head. "He didn't give me a name. When I asked why, he just told me that they thought you were into something bad. He didn't say what." Angry as he was, Dev saw the regret in Mason's face. "I just thought if it got you into trouble then I was happy to help out. Especially after what you did to me at the party."

Dev pressed the panel. It opened with a hiss. He reached inside the storage box beyond. "The party? You deserved that. You're the one who set me up to go there, after all."

Mason looked puzzled. "I didn't set you up. You just came along. . ." He flinched as he saw Dev pull something long and thin from the box.

Dev saw him flinch and laughed. "It's not a gun,

if that's what you're thinking." It was not a very enthusiastic laugh; the seriousness of the situation was too much for that. He had found his mole.

"You're a traitor, Mase. You led them in here and you knew it." He took a step closer to Mason.

Lot held up her hands to separate them. "Wait a second. Why? Why does you being here make any difference?"

Mason pulled the small pack of chewing gum from his pocket and held it up as evidence. "This. They told me once I was inside to chew a piece and stick it to the side of a computer. That was all."

Dev snatched the pack. It looked normal. He extracted the last piece of gum. It was still wrapped in silver foil. He examined it carefully. "You idiot. . ." Now Eema's inability to handle the intruders made sense.

"It's just gum. Tastes a little metallic, but. . ."

Dev ran his fingers across the gun, his eyes closed. "It's not just gum. It's a bio-virus."

He pulled a microchip from inside the wrapper. It was about the size of a pea. "And this is a portable cloaking device. That's why Eema couldn't see you."

He noticed Lot was looking at him with a now-familiar curious expression. "You know all this just by touching it?" she asked.

Dev nodded. He dropped the cloaking chip in the water and pocketed the pack of gum. He looked at Mason. "You know what a computer virus does, right? Well, our systems here are impossible to break into from outside. But inside . . . that's a little easier. You've been used as a stooge. We have a whole section here dealing with bioengineering. Forget horror novels, what they created in there . . . it's real creepy stuff. There's a real virus in the gum that's half alive, half machine. Synthesized life, they call it."

"Man-made life," said Lot. "Wow. . ."

"Your saliva activates the synth-life, then you put the gum on the computer. The virus finds a way into the system through the circuit board, bypassing any virus checkers – then it hacks the computer from the inside. It doesn't need complicated commands. All it needs to do is switch off our security systems temporarily to allow them time to get inside and do it properly." He held the incriminating stick of gum up for Lot to see. "*This* is how they bypassed Eema. Because of him!"

"I didn't know! I swear . . . I didn't know!" babbled Mason.

Dev tossed the long object he had been holding at Mason. Mason caught it out of instinct, but then reeled back, expecting it to be something harmful. He was ready to throw it into the water when Dev handed Lot another one.

"It's an aqualung so you can breathe underwater."

The gizmo looked like a harmonica. One side had a series of holes; the other was a clip that could be gripped between the teeth.

"You suck in water." Dev pointed to the holes at the front. "The oxygen is removed for you to breathe and the liquid is pushed from the sides." He indicated a pair of holes at the end of the aqualung.

Lot placed hers in her mouth and spoke as if she had a mouth full of marbles. "*'is is sho neat!*" she mumbled.

Dev stood at the edge of the platform. "They don't process nearly enough air from the water, so breathing is difficult. You'll be constantly out of breath, like being at high altitude. But at least it will keep you alive."

Dev stared at the water, then looked at Mason and Lot in turn. "I never asked you to come this far, but I need to find this Iron Fist – and whatever Eema said, I also need to rescue my uncle. You can stay here and hide, or come with me."

Mason hesitated. "I'm not a very strong swimmer."

"You don't need to swim. You just need to be able to sink." Dev slipped the aqualung into his mouth and leapt into the water.

White bubbles foamed around Dev as he sank. The cold water was a pleasant contrast to the horrors of the vacuum tube. He took a few experimental breaths through the aqualung and was relieved to discover he was sucking in cool air. The chill seeping through his body made him shiver, which in turn caused him to suck in several deep breaths. He was already struggling to breathe.

Two more splashes close by alerted him that Lot and Mason had taken the plunge too. As the curtain of bubbles cleared, he saw a range of emotions cross their faces in rapid succession – apprehension, fear, panic, then, finally, acceptance.

Of the two of them, Lot looked the more relaxed. Dev remembered an English lesson after one summer when she had written about scuba diving with her parents. Mason was the picture of uncertainty.

The water around them was as clear as glass. Two enormous black objects lay ahead and below. They were so huge that even in the crystal-clear water, the far ends disappeared in a distant blue haze. Dev motioned for the others to follow as he swam towards them.

Eventually the objects resolved themselves into a pair of huge submarines, seated on gigantic cradles that would have been in a dry dock before the security measures had activated. One of the subs resembled a dart, with the side panels forming sharp angles like a stealth fighter. The other was even bigger; the top of it was flat, and as they got closer, they could make out that they were swimming over a runway. The submarine was also an aircraft carrier.

Dev had seen both subs from the ground, when the chamber wasn't flooded, and viewing them from this new angle made them all the more impressive. He led the way between the two massive crafts. He remembered that they were oriented towards the doors leading to the next section. With any luck they would make it through before the Collector's thugs had had chance to get wet.

Dev's chest was already aching with the effort of breathing underwater. The aqualungs had been developed by the British navy. During their initial tests, divers had passed out through sheer exhaustion and subsequently drowned. Dev hadn't shared this last titbit with the others. He hoped they could pass through the next section before that became an issue.

He paused to catch his breath, hanging in the water and enjoying the sense of weightlessness. Lot caught him up and he saw a gleam of pleasure in her eyes.

Mason was several metres further back, swimming with an awkward doggy paddle. When he finally reached them, Dev pointed ahead. The tails of both subs could clearly be seen now, and so could the wall beyond. They had almost reached the far side of the chamber. Dev indicated that the door to the next zone lay to the left, out of sight.

Suddenly two shafts of light pierced through the water from above. A pair of small single-person submarines had sneaked behind them, using the vast stealth submarine for cover. The mini-subs were the size and shape of a sleek sports car and Dev recalled last seeing them stored on a shelf. He had never seen how gracefully they moved through the water.

Squinting against the light, Dev could see a grinning mercenary behind the controls of the nearest sub. A torpedo pod slid from the side of his craft, and the thug smirked, then mimed an explosion.

Kwolek was behind the waterproof canopy of the

second vehicle. As Dev watched, a pair of mechanical arms unfolded from the craft and reached for him.

He was struggling to breathe, and his movements had become sluggish through lack of oxygen. With growing dread, he realized there was no way he could escape.

CALL IN THE ELF

Sergeant Wade ducked as fragments of the sonic drill exploded with a high-pitched whine that would ring in her ears for an hour afterwards.

The drill, along with several other heavy pieces of equipment, had been airlifted in to try to access the Inventory.

Every attempt had failed.

She looked at the scorched remains of the battlefield. A couple of barns were ablaze and half the farmhouse had crumbled in on itself, but at least the enemy had been defeated with injuries to only two of her unit. They had been quickly airlifted from the scene as the remainder of the World Consortium unit secured the area.

A soldier whose fatigues were streaked with dirty snow and flecks of blood ran up to her and smartly saluted. "Ma'am, the surface is secure, but there appears to be no way to enter the Inventory from here."

She took in the soldier's name tag. "Thank you, Gamble. What about Eema?" Wade asked almost as an afterthought. Once Eema had broadcast the distress call, the computer had fallen silent, another indicator that the intruders knew exactly what they were doing.

"Not a squeak," replied Gamble. "HQ called in with a news report from Russia. Pavel Branonov is missing, along with all his notes about Project Iron Fist."

Wade frowned. Pavel Branonov used to work for the Consortium but had since retired.

Gamble continued. "A police report also states that he was seen breaking into Professor Yenin's Moscow apartment, where he stole a journal with information regarding Iron Fist."

"Yenin was responsible for creating the security here." Wade's gaze locked with the soldier's. "What was in his journal?"

"We don't know."

Sergeant Wade nodded. "Get the ELF set up. Broadcast straight down. Let's see who is listening." Extremely Low Frequency transmitters could send signals through oceans. They could transmit through solid rock, from one pole to the other if necessary. It was the only method open to them to communicate with Devon or Charles Parker, if they were still alive.

Private Gamble saluted again and walked swiftly away. Wade absently kicked at the earth beneath her boots as she watched him go, gouging a hole a few centimetres deep in the snow-covered dirt. She had no doubts her team would be able to infiltrate the Inventory and confront the intruders. But that wasn't her plan. Her plan was to sit and wait for them to come to her. . .

DEEP TROUBLE

It was impossible to avoid the submersible's claw as it struck like a cobra. Fine ropy tendrils extended from its tip and wrapped around him like anemone stingers. Dev resisted the urge to howl as his chest was crushed; he knew that would result in him drowning.

Kwolek retracted the mechanical arm, reeling Dev closer to the canopy. Out of the corner of his eye, Dev saw Lot and Mason attempting to swim for cover with the other sub in pursuit.

Dev was now face-to-face with Kwolek through the shield of the canopy. He was surprised to find that, close up, she was pretty, even with the black titanium skeleton implants. However, her dark eyes were bereft of emotion and her smile could chill a piranha.

Satisfied Dev was still breathing, Kwolek accelerated her craft, and Dev found himself soaring over the huge stealth sub, then plunging downwards so fast that a pain shot through his ears and he felt stabbing in the back of his eyeballs caused by the sudden increase in water pressure. The faster they descended, the more unbearable the pain became.

A pale light ahead made him forget the pain for an instant. At first, it was difficult to make out what he was looking at. From a distance it appeared to be a dome of glass moving along the floor. As they drew closer, Dev could see several figures walking within the dome. Then, like an optical illusion, the reality snapped into place – it wasn't a glass dome but an eight-metre half-bubble of air surrounding its occupants, who were dry and able to move normally.

Lee led the five mercenaries, who were all carrying familiar energy weapons. The Wright twins hauled a large metal case between them, covered in military-style stencilled writing: DANGER: HIGH ENERGY.

In the middle of the armed escort walked Charles Parker. Alongside him was a robot rolling along on caterpillar tracks. It looked like something from the 1970s, an old bomb-disposal robot. However, the shimmering device mounted on top of it was much more recent: it was producing the field that repelled the water, creating the half-bubble.

The group turned in unison as Kwolek's mini-sub drew nearer. The surface of the air bubble distorted the view, exactly like looking into a pool of water. Charles Parker squinted as the sub's arm extended towards them. It was holding something.

"Devon?" Charles Parker exclaimed as Dev was thrust into the air bubble.

Dev found it an odd sensation suddenly transitioning from the cold water into the warm, humid air bubble, like diving in reverse. One moment he was fighting for breath and suffering acute pressure – the next he was hanging from the claw several metres above the ground *inside* the sanctuary of the air bubble, while Kwolek's sub hovered in the water above them. The pain in his ears instantly subsided.

He looked sheepishly at his uncle. "Hi."

Charles Parker's eyes darted between his nephew and Lee. "Is this your idea of a rescue?"

Lee slowly circled Dev. "Ah yes, the infamous

nephew. Loved that Trojan you put in Eema – classy. You've been causing no end of trouble." He indicated to the submarine holding Dev aloft. "Kwolek there is desperate to crush the life out of you for what you did to her. Do you think I should allow her?" Dev avoided his gaze. "I thought not. Release him."

The claw lowered Dev to the floor. He landed hard, twisting his ankle. The aqualung dropped from his mouth and slid across the floor.

"Check he has no weapons on him."

Two henchmen dragged Dev to his feet and one performed a perfunctory pat-down, using the tips of his fingers to find any concealed weapons. He stopped at the pack of gum in Dev's pocket, but quickly dismissed it.

"The kid has nothing," he said, a little surprised.

Dev was even more surprised. Evidently the man was either not there when Mason was recruited, or dumb. Or possibly both.

"You won't get the Iron Fist," he said with more confidence than he felt.

The way Lee paused gave him hope. "Really? And what do you know of the Iron Fist?"

The mercenary released Dev. He winced as he put

weight on his twisted ankle. "It's Nikola Tesla's old invention. What do you want to know?"

Lee regarded Dev with suspicion. Before he could reply, his radio earpiece crackled to life. In the silence of the bubble, Dev could just hear a voice.

"Sir, we have lost contact with the surface team. Last transmissions indicated that Consortium forces had overwhelmed them."

Dev met Charles Parker's gaze. They both knew that meant the task force would attempt to storm the Inventory. The flicker of hope grew in Dev's chest, but he could see disappointment in his uncle's face. Was it because Dev had been caught? Or was he disappointed that Dev had been forced to call for help?

As usual, Dev felt he could do nothing right. He held in his anger as he noticed they had reached the large door leading to the next zone. The air bubble pushed against it, clearing the water away.

"That is not unexpected," said Lee without the slightest concern for the team he had lost on the surface. "The World Consortium will implement their usual procedures, which is what I'm counting on."

Dev felt sick at the idea that everything was unfolding just as the thieves had anticipated. He hoped Lot and

Mason were still free. He peered through the bubble, but the smooth surface refracted the light, making it difficult to see anything further than Kwolek's sub. What if the other sub had caught them . . . or worse?

"Get this door open!" Lee barked.

The twins lugged their case closer to the door. They heaved the lid off and began assembling the complicated device contained within.

Dev reached into his pocket – and stopped as a soldier raised his gun in warning.

"Easy, kid."

Dev raised one hand to indicate he was unarmed, while he slowly took the packet of chewing gum from his pocket. "Easy yourself," he said as he unwrapped his last strip and popped it into his mouth, putting the silver foil wrapper back in his pocket. "The only danger here is to my teeth."

While Lee's attention was focused on the door, he stepped closer to his uncle and whispered: "Can you swim?" It was crazy, Dev realized, how little he really knew about Charles Parker.

Charles raised his handcuffs. "I won't be charging into the water, if that's what you have in mind." There was irritation in his voice.

Dev raised a questioning eyebrow at the sight of the cuffs.

"I had no option but to surrender." Charles glared at Dev. "I sacrificed myself to buy you time. What a waste that was! And stop chewing while I'm talking to you. It's a filthy habit."

Every word hurt Dev. Even as they faced imminent danger, his uncle couldn't stop his petty complaints. Dev now wondered why he had even considered trying to save him. Iron Fist – that was the plan. Get it, get out. Tough luck if his uncle was left behind.

Fuming, he spat the gum at the shield generator device mounted on the robot. It was a perfect hit – just as he had hoped. "Happy?"

"Do I look happy?"

"I don't know, I've never seen that before," hissed Dev.

His uncle glowered. "I don't need rescuing, Devon. Are you too blind to see? They used me as bait to lure you here!"

Dev blinked. "But why would they want me? I'm not special."

His uncle's face suddenly softened, and for a moment he saw the caring face of the man who had raised him.

It was almost foreign; certainly Dev hadn't seen it for many years.

"Oh, Devon," he sighed. "If only you knew. . ."

There was a flash from beyond the confines of the bubble. Dev and his uncle spun round. Something had struck Kwolek's submarine from behind – shunting the vehicle forward and through the wall of the bubble.

Dev and Charles Parker flung themselves against the far wall to avoid the plummeting craft. With no water to support it, the sub landed with a terrible crunch. The carbon-fibre hull split open and slid across the floor, scattering the twins and Lee before it slammed into the wall, crushing the machine they had been building.

Smashing the fractured canopy aside with her bionic arm, Kwolek rolled out of the wreckage, cut and bruised. Her eyes locked on to Dev. She scowled and took a menacing step towards him before being restrained by Lee.

Dev scrambled on all fours for his aqualung. He picked it up and turned to his uncle. "You never said if you could swim." His eyes shot to the robot as he jammed the aqualung in his mouth.

Charles Parker followed Dev's gaze. The gum had

landed on the shield generator that was creating the air pocket. He instantly knew what Dev's plan was.

"NO!" bellowed Charles Parker.

It was too late. Dev sprinted to the edge of the bubble and dived into the vertical wall of water. It was just like diving into a pool but without the splash. He kicked hard to distance himself from the air pocket and looked around for the cause of Kwolek's woes.

Dev knew he didn't have a choice. He just prayed that Charles Parker could swim.

The second sub was hovering in the water next to him. The paintwork on the front was scuffed from the impact of Kwolek's machine. Dev was baffled as to why its pilot hadn't prevented the crash.

As Dev swam around to get a better look inside the cockpit, he was surprised to see Mason was at the controls, grinning like an idiot. He gave Dev a thumbs up.

Dev swam towards the sub and gripped the hull just as the bio-virus in the gum infiltrated the circuitry on the shield generator and shut the device down.

The air pocket collapsed and a wall of water tumbled down on Charles Parker, Lee and his team.

The surge dragged the sub towards it, with Dev

clinging to its hull – but Mason opened the throttle and pulled them away. Dev looked around frantically for a sign of his uncle. Then with horror he remembered Charles Parker's cuffs.

Had he just killed his uncle?

Mason brought the sub to a halt and Dev saw Lot swimming over. Reaching the sub, she put her arms around him – was she that delighted to see him? Even with the horror and guilt whirling in his mind, it felt good.

However, Dev knew they were far from safe. Lee would soon have the door open and leap ahead of them. And that door was the only way onwards.

Or was it?

Dev quickly swam to the sub, pulling Lot with him. He secured his arm around a pipe and indicated Lot should do the same. Then he knocked on the canopy to get Mason's attention and pointed to the floor.

Several metres away was a covered grid the size of a garage door, with the word "PURGE" stencilled on in a military fashion.

Dev patted the missile pods, then indicated to the grid. Inside the cramped cockpit, Mason nodded in understanding.

With a quick buzz from the sub's rotors, Mason positioned the submarine and fired a torpedo straight at the grid. His aim was perfect.

The moment it struck there was a roaring sound and the sub was sucked towards the breach. Dev held on to the sub for dear life and realized that was exactly what Lot was doing to him.

They spiralled towards the grid as if entering a black hole, building speed with every second. Then they were plunged into darkness – sucked down the giant plughole as thousands of tons of water poured from the Blue Zone.

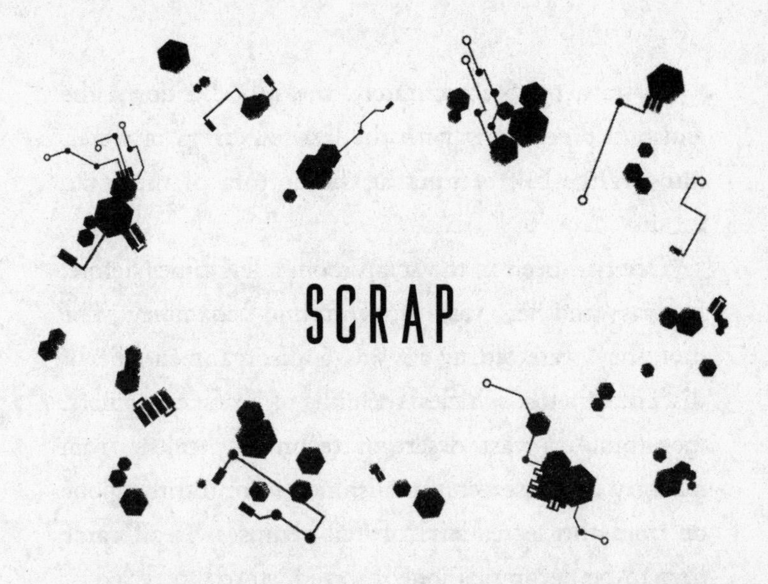

SCRAP

Dev watched as Mason doubled over and loudly heaved his guts. Surely, he thought, there was nothing left to give?

Lot scrunched her nose against the vile smell. Like Mason, she was feeling delicate after the violent washing-machine spin they had endured. They had been bucked in every direction in the darkness for what had seemed like an eternity.

Eventually the massive column of water that had been pushing them along had receded as it siphoned through grilles in the tunnel. Then the sub, with Dev and Lot clinging on, had been spat out into the scrap room.

Or rather more accurately, the sub slid down the end of a pipe, along with the last few dregs of water, into a large hill of junk at the bottom of the scrap room.

Dev had been in the scrap room a few times before. It was another vast underground chamber. The half they were sitting in was a disorganized pile of discarded items: vehicles, the hulls of boats, computers, monitors – a vast desert of technology taken from military and research establishments around the globe or from the secret lairs of evil geniuses. It all came here to be decommissioned, sorted, stored, recycled or destroyed.

Dev had forgotten that the drainage grid in the complex was filtered. Any tiny item of potential value found its way into this room. That way no tiny gadget or microchip could be accidentally lost down the sink.

It had saved their lives.

In the other half of the chamber were orderly stacks of items that were in the middle of being processed – a time-consuming operation that Charles Parker conducted with Eema. Every now and again he came across a gem. It was in a haul of scrap from a decommissioned Russian military base that the Iron Fist had been discovered.

Mason stood up and stretched, breathing in deeply. "I needed that," he sighed. He studied Dev. "You OK? You look worse than I feel."

Dev smiled. "Thanks for saving me back there." The words came out with difficulty, but he had to clear his conscience. "I'm sorry about what I said. About calling you a traitor."

A half smile tugged the corner of Mason's mouth. "I think I owed you."

Lot clapped her hands. "Excellent! Friends at last!"

Dev and Mason spoke at the same time: "I wouldn't go that far!"

All three of them burst into laughter. It helped ease a little of the guilt Dev was feeling about his uncle.

"You should have seen Mase," said Lot, giddy with excitement. "That sub chased us so we headed straight for some shelves—"

"Well, I followed her," Mason interjected modestly. "She's like a flippin' mermaid in the water."

"Yeah. Unfortunately he's more like a very slow whale." Mason shot her a playful scowl. "Anyway, the idiot inside came after us. Well, me, it came after *me*."

"Yeah, straight past me. I was hiding behind some junk—"

Dev couldn't resist adding a jibe. "That I believe." He was surprised that his heart wasn't quite in it.

Lot continued. "So it followed between some shelves." She held both hands close together to indicate how narrow the gap was. "And got stuck right there."

"Right in front of me," Mason added proudly. "I saw a lever right there." He indicated it was within reach. "And emergency release. So I yanked it and – BOOM! Bubbles everywhere!"

"He'd only gone and ejected the pilot!" Lot laughed so hard there were tears in her eyes. Mason joined in, belly laughing as he mimed the guy shooting to the surface. Dev could only watch them as they recovered from the fit of giggles.

Mason composed himself. "So I swam into the cockpit. Found a lever that resealed the cockpit and drained the water out. Then I took it. It's so easy to drive, like playing a computer game."

"And since he's such a lousy swimmer, I thought it was best that he drive," said Lot, winking at Mason. "We dislodged it from the shelf—"

"And came back to rescue you," Mason finished.

"Impressive," said Dev, and he meant it. "I suppose that officially makes us a team?"

Lot nodded sagely. "I think it does." Then her voice lowered. "I'm sure your uncle will be OK. I saw people swimming towards the surface."

Dev faked a smile. He knew he wouldn't be able to shift his guilt that easily.

Lot sat down beside him and laid a hand on his arm. "He'll be OK. Unfortunately I think the thieves will be too. What did your uncle say to you?"

Dev stared at his feet. "My uncle looked like he hated me. As if all of this was my fault. He seemed to think the Collector was using him as bait to get to me. I think . . . I know this sounds crazy . . . but I get the impression they think I am linked to the Iron Fist. One of the guys asked me about it."

Lot frowned. "How is that possible? You hadn't even heard about it before today."

"I wish we could plug into Eema; then I might be able to find out more or at least send a message to the rescue team."

"What rescue team?" said Mason sharply.

"The World Consortium has sent a task force. They've secured the farm above but can't get down here. They're using ELFs."

Lot giggled. "Are you trying to tell me elves and leprechauns are real too?"

Dev laughed. "ELFs – Extremely Low Frequency radio waves. That's what we use here when my uncle needs to talk to me." He waved his wrist where his watch used to be. "They can transmit data through water and rock."

Lot stood up, suddenly excited. "So if they are trying to talk to whoever's down here we can respond, right?"

Dev sighed. "Only if we had an ELF transmitter. Without my watch. . ." He shrugged.

Lot clipped him across the head.

"OW! What did you do that for?"

"For a genius you are really dumb sometimes. I mean, I'm thinking if there was just *some place* we could get parts to put an ELF receiver together." She extended her arms, gesturing to the room. "Come on! You're smarter than me and even I can work this one out."

Dev looked around the room. The scrap room was filled with *everything* he would need. He stood up, suddenly excited.

"I'm not smarter than you," he said with a growing smile. "I just know lots more useless things. And I take being dumb to a whole new level."

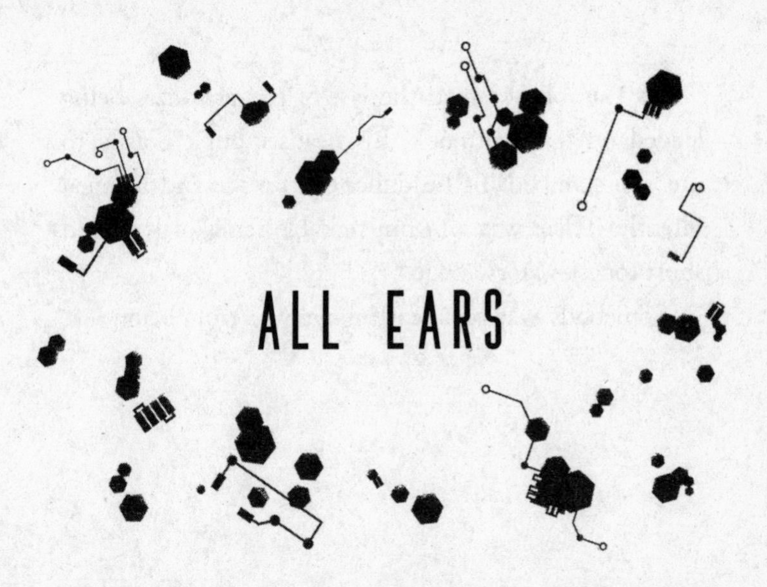

ALL EARS

Private Gamble sat at a large ELF radio control panel that was covered in touchscreens and images of flowing waveforms that were broadcasting ELF signals. He was listening for the faintest reply. Rather than connect to a transmitter aerial or an array of satellite dishes, cables had been set up to run to several large domes bolted into the snowy ground. They were the powerful resonators that created signals so low the human ear was incapable of hearing them. Some animals could, and Gamble smiled at an encounter he'd had in Africa. Dozing off one night while using the ELF array, he had awoken to find himself surrounded by dozens of curious elephants.

As Gamble watched the last of the prisoners being loaded on to a Chinook, his headset burst noisily to life. He clamped his headphones in place and listened intently. There was an unmistakable series of long and short tones – Morse code.

Somebody was broadcasting an SOS from below.

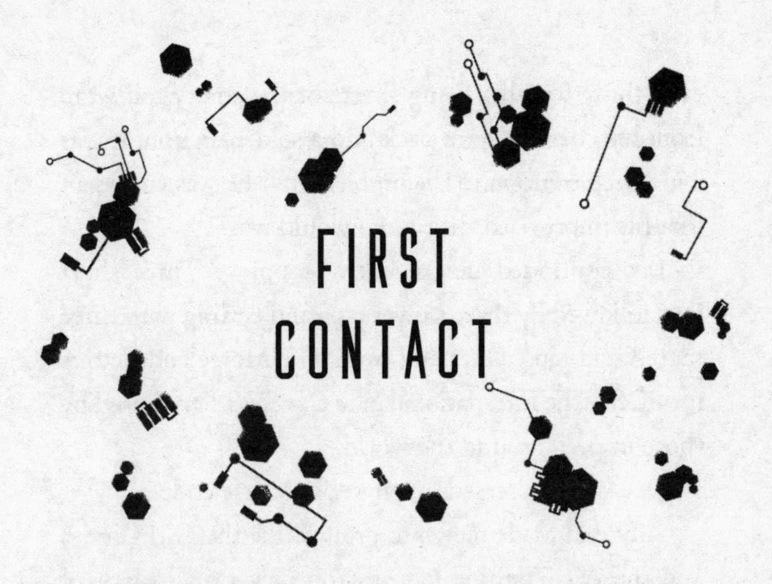

FIRST CONTACT

Dev watched as Lot tapped carefully on the computer touchpad. He had hardwired it to an old transmitter he'd taken from an unusual industrial machine they had uncovered among the junk. The front of the machine was a large pointed drilling bit attached to a yellow cylindrical body in which two people could sit. Dev thought it had been designed by some eccentric maverick to try and reach the earth's core. Most importantly, though, it had a 1940s Bakelite radio that he was able to cannibalize.

He made a quick repair to a set of giant speakers, presumably discarded from a rock concert, and connected everything together using slivers of the empty foil wrap from his chewing gum pack and a soldering iron. It was a low-tech solution to the problem, but he was confident that his improvised ELF radio would work.

Lot continued her repetitive tapping. Three short taps followed by three slower taps and ending with three more rapid taps. Over and over. The Morse code letters for SOS – the international *Save Our Souls* signal used by those in peril around the world.

Dev was impressed. "You know Morse code?"

"My dad made me go to groups like the Girl Guides and the Air Training Corps. You pick up all kinds of useless stuff."

"Useless stuff that may just save our lives."

"What about you? It looks like you can fix anything. Who does that?"

Mason laughed. "I would love you to come to my house. The amount of broken junk we have … you could fix it all and I could make a fortune on eBay."

Dev felt embarrassed; he'd never been lavished with this much praise before.

"My uncle taught me the basics…" he mumbled. He didn't really know how to explain his gift, so any excuse would have to do.

"You talk a lot about your uncle," Lot said with as much tact as she could muster. "What about your parents?"

"I didn't know my dad, and my mum vanished a long time ago."

"Vanished?"

"My uncle says she just left with no explanation. He doesn't really talk about it." Dev looked into the middle distance, trying to recall any fragment about his mother he could. "I vaguely remember her, but sometimes it's like a dream. I can't really make out her face ... or even the sound of her voice... Maybe it's just my imagination." He lapsed into silence.

"Surely he has some family pictures," pressed Lot. "So you can see what she looks like?"

"He's not the most sentimental man in the world. I don't think he does photos."

"Hey," Mason interrupted. "The line is freaking out."

He pointed to the circular green screen of the ancient oscilloscope Dev had mounted on the radio. The line, which had been steadily flat, was now wobbling in a series of jagged peaks and troughs.

Dev nudged Lot excitedly. "Somebody's responding

to us!" He twisted the volume up, but it was already on maximum. "Why aren't we hearing them?"

With steady fingers, he traced his improvised wiring. Everything seemed to be in place – until he discovered a pair of wires he had twisted together had come undone. He reattached them, getting a mild electric shock. It was worth it, as a faint woman's voice, wreathed in static, now came from the speakers.

"Come in. Repeat. This is Sergeant Wade from the World Consortium task force to whoever is transmitting the SOS; please come in."

Lot handed Dev the microphone, salvaged from a battered walkie-talkie Mason had found.

"Sergeant Wade, we hear you." Dev's voice trembled with excitement.

"Devon? Is that you?" came the voice.

Dev frowned. "How do you know my name?"

Wade laughed with relief. "We know all about you and your uncle, Devon. Part of our mission has been to watch over the Inventory."

"Well, we're glad to hear you! And by the way, it's Dev, not Devon."

"Dev it is. Is your uncle with you?"

"No. I'm with Lot and Mason, two fr . . . friends

from school." The word *friend* felt alien on his tongue. "We made it to the scrap room."

"Is your uncle still alive?"

Dev hesitated. He hoped so. He couldn't live with himself otherwise. "Yes. They have him as a hostage."

"It's imperative that you keep away from the thieves. Understand?"

"That's what we're trying to do. But they're armed. They've taken down Eema and have already broken into the Blue Zone. They're after the Iron Fist."

The tone of Wade's voice changed. "What do you know about Iron Fist?"

"Only what I need to – which is naff all!" snapped Dev. "Eema told me to stop them from getting it."

"That's exactly what you must do."

Before Dev could reply, Mason spoke up. "Wait a minute. Us? Aren't you the hotshot soldiers? Why aren't you swooping down here and saving us from the mess?"

"I assume that's Mason Kermit McDermott?"

Dev and Lot couldn't suppress smiles. *Kermit?*

Mason scowled at them. "My mum liked the name."

"No wonder you have anger issues," sniggered Dev.

Wade continued. "Well, Mason, it's simple. We can't

get in. The Shadow Helix team have been very thorough about that. But you can get out, and that means using—"

"The teleporter in the Red Zone," finished Dev.

"Exactly," said Wade.

Dev sighed. That was typical Inventory logic – you had to go deeper into danger in order to get out.

Wade continued. "Look at it this way: you are already in the scrap room. The Red Zone is one of the rooms connected to that. Once you're in there, out you come."

"You make it sound so simple," Dev replied drily.

Wade hesitated before continuing. "There are just a couple of hurdles." Dev closed his eyes and remained silent. "We need you to find the Iron Fist and bring it out with you. It is imperative that the thieves don't get their hands on it."

"How hard can that be?" said Lot brightly. She was relieved their ordeal was almost over.

"You'll be surprised," Dev muttered under his breath.

Wade continued. "It is important that you *don't* activate Iron Fist, no matter what happens. Just bring it out with you. And don't touch anything else in there. Items in the Red Zone are considered dangerous for a reason."

Mason looked at the others in surprise. "You mean the rest of the stuff *isn't*?"

"And finally." Wade's voice dropped a little. "The intruders neutralized Eema so she wouldn't get in their way. That means once you are in the Red Zone, the husk will be nothing more than an automated attack dog. No AI, no reasoning with it; the Inventory's basic security system will assume you're the enemy and she won't be around to put it straight. If you are in the Red Zone – you will be destroyed."

THE FINAL DOOR

As soon as the transmission was over, Dev and Lot set to work combing through the scrap room, gathering items that they could use, or, rather, assemble into something useful.

Lot watched in awed silence as Dev laid the various components on the ground and, after looking at them for a minute or so, began pulling pieces off and slotting them into one another. His hands moved swiftly and he didn't appear to need to think about what he was doing.

"I'm not stupid, Dev," she finally said. "There's no way your uncle could have taught you to do that." She remembered the way he'd run his fingers across the door lock in the canteen. "There's something more. When you touch things . . . you control them."

Dev stopped what he was doing. "No, not control them. I can *sense* how they work. Synaesthesia."

She shook her head. "Never heard of them. What kind of music do they play?"

Dev made a face. "It's a neurological condition I have. It kinda mixes your senses up so you hear sounds when you touch something, or see things when you hear a noise." Lot looked at him as if expecting a punch line to a joke. Dev sighed. "Some people can look at numbers and see colours flashing in their mind. They find doing maths as easy as mixing the colours together. They're capable of doing massive equations in their head without thinking about it."

"Far out," said Lot, although it was clear she didn't fully understand.

"Others can feel a shape or a texture and they hear a sound. So instead of touching a toy car and thinking it's kinda square with round wheels, they hear a series of tones that, *to them*, perfectly describe the shape."

He laughed when he saw Lot staring at him. "I know. It sounds totally bonkers, but it's true. My condition is a little of both. I look at electronics or mechanics and I see colours and hear tones. Almost like music. If the colours are jarring or the music sounds off-key, then I know the device is broken. If I get the colours and sounds to work in harmony then I can fix it."

"I don't want to say that sounds weird, but. . ."

"I know. It took me years to realize that it wasn't normal. Basically that's why I can figure out how things work and fix them. I just feel my way along, which is how I can make things like this." He held up the device he had been working on while talking. It was long, like a bazooka, and both ends were wide like funnels. "It's a non-lethal weapon, of course." He balanced it on Lot's shoulder.

"What does it do?" Lot aimed it at Mason, who had his back to them as he prodded a piece of wreckage.

Dev angled the barrel away from Mason. "I said non-lethal, but I'm pretty sure it will hurt. It's an AirCannon." He pointed to the rear end. "Air is sucked through here at high speed." He ran his hand down to the middle. "It's compressed in a chamber here. And when you pull the trigger—"

Lot pulled the trigger. It sounded like a champagne cork popping, only much bassier. A shimmering sphere of compressed air shot across the scrap until it hit the remains of an old four-by-four and exploded with a bang, flipping the vehicle on to its roof.

Mason jumped to his feet and looked accusingly at Lot.

"Wow," she said with a grin. "That was neat."

"I got the idea from their sonic guns. With any luck we won't have to use it, but it's better to be safe than sorry."

They joined Mason and together gazed across the massive space. It was so cavernous that the humidity had created its own microclimate – one of a foggy haze that almost shrouded the far wall from view and hung like low cloud. They could just make out the dark smudge of another circular doorway so large that it could swallow a building.

"That's the Red Zone."

"And you've never been there before?" said Mason.

"Never."

"So you don't know what will be waiting for us?"

"Nope."

"Or how to get in?"

"Not a clue."

Lot and Mason exchanged a resigned look. "Then what are we waiting for?" Lot said. "Let's break into the most secure vault in the most secure building in the world."

The closer they came to the vault door, the further Mason and Lot hung back. Like the other portals, this door was circular, but it was far larger – so large that the top was hidden in the humid mist. A small hand scanner was mounted to the right of the door. Dev studied it, but didn't dare touch it.

"Surely it's worth trying your palm print?" Mason suggested.

Dev shook his head. "My uncle made it very clear that I was never to go in here, no matter what. At best, I touch that scanner and the Collector will know exactly where we are."

Lot looked nervous. "And the worst-case scenario is. . .?"

"Eema has been overridden so we become targets."

Mason forced a laugh, although it sounded more than a little fearful. "So what? We beat those goons back there. We can beat your souped-up tin can."

"But in this case it will be a tin can armed with weapons so terrible that the World Consortium decreed no military could ever use them."

"That's one tin can with attitude," said Lot.

Dev saw Mason's face pale, his bravado slipping away. "So why are we doing this again? Shouldn't we just hide? I mean, who's going to blame us if we can't stop them getting the Iron Fist?"

"We're doing it because no matter how scary things have been so far, Iron Fist is supposed to be far worse."

A deep boom suddenly resonated across the hangar. They turned around and peered into in the distant haze.

"That was the door to the Blue Zone," whispered Dev. "They're in here."

"Can you use your synaesthesia power to open this door?" said Lot, turning back to the portal.

"It's not a superpower," Dev said. "I can't hack into computers with my mind."

A thought struck him. He began to back away from the door so he could see the whole thing.

"What are you doing?" Lot hissed. "It's not going to take them that long to get over here!"

"I'm taking a step back to see the whole problem," said Dev. "My uncle sorts through all this trash on his own. Do you know how he does it?"

Dev peered up to the ceiling, which was a cloud of

haze with powerful spotlights puncturing through like miniature suns.

"No idea," said Lot.

Dev smiled. "Then let me show you."

GIVE HIM A HAND

Lee stared at the Red Zone door and let out a low whistle. "That's one big sucker. It makes you wonder what's really behind it." He turned to look at the team around him. Everybody had gathered to enter the final portal, but they were all keeping a wary distance.

Charles Parker shrugged. "The most powerful items ever created. Although looks can be deceiving."

Lee thumbed his watch; the image of the Collector instantly appeared. "Sir, we're at the final door."

The Collector sounded impatient. "At last. And the children?"

For the first time Lee felt a cold sweat trickle down

his back, and he hesitated. "They are . . . out of the way."

The Collector's silence was threatening. Lee continued nervously, "Once we are through, the team was wondering exactly how we are expected to complete the final phase."

"Find Iron Fist and have it brought to me. We shall rendezvous outside. After that, everything will take care of itself."

The Collector vanished. Lee took a deep breath and noticed that Charles Parker was looking at him with the faintest hint of a smile.

"What're you smirking at?" snarled Lee. He jerked his thumb at the door. "Open it up."

Fermi stepped in front of the palm scanner. The innocuous black metal plate offered no instructions. She pulled a small box from her backpack, about the size of a shoebox.

"OK, Pops." She gestured Charles Parker forward. "Come here."

Charles knew it was pointless to resist. With a bemused look, he joined her. She placed his hand in a circular hole at one end of the box. "Just relax."

There was a blue flash from within the box and

Charles rapidly withdrew his hand. A pinkish puddle formed in a tray on top of the box. It took a moment for Charles to realize that it was a patch of human skin. "You are making a 3D printout of my hand?"

"Every fingerprint, scar, ridge and whorl," Fermi confirmed. "But not just a scan..."

They watched as an entire human hand formed from the top of the machine, the wrist nothing more than a curved lump of flesh. Fermi picked it up, and used it to wave at Charles. The fingers flexed and moved. He was impressed – and it took a lot to impress Charles Parker.

"It's an exact *living* copy. Well, living for a few minutes. This is the next generation beyond cloning. We can print people now."

Charles Parker couldn't hold back his astonishment. "Incredible!"

Lee shook his head. "You have been down here far too long, Prof. The world above is moving faster than the junk you've amassed here." He took the hand from Fermi. The fingers tried to grab him; it was like holding an angry crab.

"My orders are to keep you alive as long as possible. Somebody up there must care about you." Lee waved the appendage at Charles. "But that doesn't mean you can't still give us a helping hand."

He passed the printed hand to a mercenary, who then carefully placed it against the palm scanner. A laser scanned the hand, causing it to twitch. For a second the plate turned green and Eema's voice spoke out. "Professor Charles Parker identified." Then a powerful electric shock surged through the plate. There was a sharp crack and the mercenary was vaporized.

The sudden violence shocked Charles. It took a moment for Lee to recover his composure.

"Wow. Looks like your own security system wants you dead." The old man's bewildered expression made Lee laugh. "It seems there are some people who know more about the Inventory than you do. What if some miscreants broke in here –" he gestured to his team "– and used you to override every lock? That's not very secure, is it? So the moment it thinks you're aiding and abetting the enemy –" he mimed an explosion "– then you're suddenly part of the problem."

Fermi frowned. "So if you knew that, what did you hope that would achieve?"

Lee shrugged. "The fail-safe." He nodded to the wall.

The door suddenly *moved* along the wall. The

entire portal drifted, without leaving a hole, as if it were nothing more than a flat image moving across a screen. As they watched, three more doors spiralled into existence, one half a metre from the ground, another two stories up, with the third somewhere between.

Charles smiled knowingly as Lee looked between the new portals. He wagged a finger as he realized what he was looking at. "Got it – holographic projections, right?"

"They are projections of a kind," said Charles. "Solid-matter projections. Only one leads into the Red Zone, and no, I don't know which. The other three are real doors in the Inventory, but I assure you *they* lead to certain death."

"It also means that brat nephew of yours hasn't got through, right?" Lee sniggered. "The electric shock, this matter projection, none of it would have kicked in if he had already broken through. So we're ahead for once."

Charles's smile made Lee hesitate. His eyes darted around the scrapheap, searching for movement. "Which means they could be dogging our heels."

Lee jerked his head the way they had come. The mercenaries got his hint and readied their weapons as they scanned the hills of trash leading to the door they had entered through.

It was utterly silent.

"Maybe they just gave up?" said Volta. He took a step forward. The room was humid; the designers had evidently thought that a scrapyard didn't require expensive air conditioning. Beads of sweat dripped into Volta's eyes. He rapidly blinked – and through the tears he almost missed the object dropping at high speed through the mist above.

Volta saw that it was an enormous claw, the kind traditionally used in junkyards, except this one had snaking tentacle fingers that allowed it to grab objects of any shape without much effort.

Three figures were perched on top of the claw, clinging to the thick metal cable that rapidly lowered them.

Lee pointed and yelled. "It's them! Shoot them down!"

Volta struggled to lock on to his target through his streaming eyes. He blindly fired – his sonic blast tearing chunks from the flailing tentacles. He wiped his eyes with his wrists and took aim again – in time to see the claw was almost over them. The tentacles were thrashing randomly, forming a shield from the troops firing below.

The flailing mechanical limbs struck two of the

mercenaries. Ducking for cover, Charles Parker heard their ribs crack as they were flung across the chamber.

Another volley of sonic blasts missed the descending claw and vanished into the mist above, striking unseen girders which came tumbling down moments later, crushing more mercenaries.

Despite the chaos unfolding around him, Charles Parker could only watch with the whisper of a smile on his face. Dev was showing some astonishing ingenuity, surely a product of the excellent education he had provided for his nephew.

Maybe the boy wasn't such a failure after all...

CHOOSE A DOOR

Dev clung for his life on to the telescoping cable as sonic blasts shot past and ceiling girders fell down around him. His eyes were tightly shut and his stomach was lurching from the rapid descent.

"You can open your eyes now," said Lot, nudging him.

It had been Dev's idea for them to ascend on one of the scrapyard's many claws that hung across the ceiling, used for lifting particularly large items – from cars to ships. The ever-present shroud of mist kept them hidden from view, providing the perfect hiding place.

The only problem was that Dev had completely

failed to foresee the effect it would have on his vertigo. It had been a far worse experience than climbing the shelving racks and he'd kept his eyes glued shut from the moment they had ascended. That had resulted in him accidentally leaning on the control that dropped them down on top of the thieves.

He felt a sharp elbow in his ribs and heard Lot again. "Dev! We need to get off this thing!"

Dev held his breath and opened his eyes. They were only a storey or so above the junkyard, but Dev still felt his head swim. His palms were slick with sweat. The entire claw reverberated as the sonic pulses, fired from below, struck the titanium tentacles. He fought the nausea in his stomach as Lot's voice rose in his conscience.

"Dev? Focus! Which door?"

Dev forced his eyes open. He studied the matter-projected doors. Eema's advice on accessing the zone had been horribly cryptic.

Just then he spotted logos etched on to the portal's hand scanners. Each was different. A circle, a square, a triangle – then he saw a hexagon.

"Rule of six," he muttered. "That's got to be it." The door was to the right and just above them. He pointed. "There!"

Mason moved Dev away from the controls. "Don't sit on anything else!"

"It's the heights. . ." said Dev feebly. He had jury-rigged hacking into the claw's actuators, a system usually controlled via Charles Parker's mobile phone. It had taken Dev just two minutes, running his hands over the circuits and complex hydraulics, in order to figure out how to rework the system.

Mason circled the joystick backwards and to the right. The claw moved so quickly that their stomachs jolted as they were thrown against the main supporting girder.

"Ram it!" Dev screamed.

Mason pivoted the claw around and swung it straight for the doorway. The claw gained speed – accelerating straight for the closed door.

"Hold on!" Mason yelled – then closed his eyes.

Dev didn't blink, but Lot and Mason both threw their hands over their heads for protection as the claw ploughed into the door.

There was no impact.

Instead, the door budged like a thin rubber sheet – and the claw passed effortlessly into the room beyond, silencing the howls of frustration from the thieves below. . .

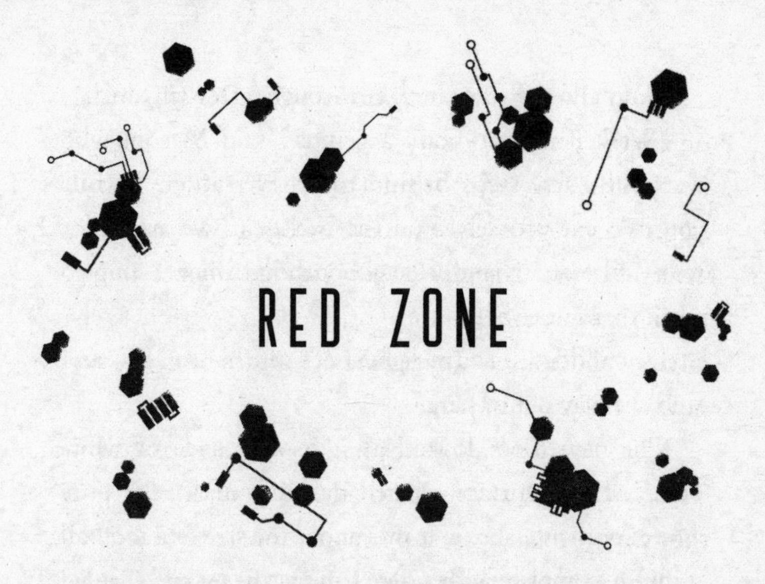

RED ZONE

Dev cheered victoriously as the claw scraped across the floor of the new chamber, trailing a fountain of sparks. Lot and Mason leapt off, their legs shaking.

"Was the door just an optical illusion or something?" asked Mason.

"Liquid metal," Dev answered. "Solid to everything, but not to these." He patted the claw. "I remembered my uncle telling me that the security systems were designed to keep people out, but the mechanical structures like these still needed to work."

Lot was ahead on this. "So the security system would detect this claw and know it belonged to the Inventory..."

“And allow it to pass right through,” Dev finished.

“Well, isn’t everybody a genius,” said Mason, who was still a few steps behind the conversation. “While you two pat yourselves on the back, can we assume it won’t take our friendly neighbourhood thieves long to work that out either?”

Dev nodded. “You’re right. Let’s get the Iron Fist and find the way out of here.”

The new room looked as if it was made of white plastic. Every surface seemed dazzling under the pure white spotlights above. It was about the size of a football stadium, complete with a tiered area at the far end that led to a dome of what looked like interlocking metal spars.

Rather than the usual racks of storage they had become accustomed to, boxy cabins lined the periphery, like sleek modern sheds. Inventory exhibits were displayed in their own areas, each cordoned off with a pulsing energy shield that distorted the view of the contents into nothing more than a mass of pixels. It was like looking into a sandstorm or a Magic Eye autostereogram picture – the exhibit only came into focus once you’d stopped and squinted.

“Which one is the Iron Fist?” said Lot, urgency in her voice as she glanced at the doorway behind them.

Dev hurried from exhibit to exhibit, pausing to squint through each energy shield. Every so often he would murmur *wow*, before hurrying to the next. Lot and Mason followed.

"I don't get it," muttered Mason. "I don't see a thing."

"Nor me." As hard as she tried to focus her eyes to see beyond the shield, Lot couldn't pick out the objects either.

"You're not trying hard enough." Dev suddenly stopped at a plinth, the energy shield clouding the object on the upper portion of it.

"This is it." He sounded disappointed. "It doesn't look so spectacular, does it?"

Lot and Mason joined him. Try as they might, they couldn't see the object beyond.

"What does it look like?" Lot asked.

But Dev had turned away from the Iron Fist. He was looking along the row of cabins. Each door sported a variety of symbols, some of which the children recognized – the three segments around a circle declaring *radiation*; the pincer-like circles denoting a *biohazard* – and others that were unfamiliar. Dev was drawn towards a cabin marked as a biohazard. He took a few steps closer to it.

Mason raised his hands helplessly. "Dev, mate, what the heck're you doing? If this is the Iron Fist, let's just grab it and go."

"I've been here before," Dev said in a low voice.

Lot frowned. "I thought you hadn't been in this section?"

"I haven't . . . at least, I thought I hadn't. But this." He pointed at the cabin doorway. "This looks familiar."

"How is that possible?" said Lot gently.

"Maybe you had your memory wiped," joked Mason.

Dev ignored him and stepped up to the door. There was no code. No palm scanner. Just a simple button to open it. A sense of familiarity nagged at him; he could almost hear whispering voices encouraging him inside.

Dev reached out to press the button. The door swished open, and the lights in the room beyond automatically flared to life. Without looking back at his friends, Dev entered.

The room was no bigger than a classroom, and it looked like one too. A row of benches were filled with clinical equipment, microscopes and old computers. Large monitors hung on the wall, their dark screens reflecting Dev's image as he entered.

He didn't hear the door slide closed behind him but

he felt the change in air pressure in his ears. Whatever biological hazard was kept in here needed its own air supply, and he suspected it was linked to the four large glass cylinders filled with liquid. They were big enough to hold a person inside. Which was exactly what they were doing.

GOOD BREEDING

Four bodies, a little smaller than Dev, were curled in foetal positions, suspended in the liquid. Their eyes were closed. It wasn't until one of them jerked that Dev realized they were *alive.*

Dev felt a sick feeling in the pit of his stomach. He had often wondered what occupied his uncle in the bowels of the Inventory.

Now he knew.

His uncle was just as much a monster as the thieves or the Collector. Dev knew, *just knew,* that this was where he had come from. Eema's words echoed in his mind:

This is what you were bred for...

This was where he was *made.*

SHOWDOWN

Dev ran from the macabre chamber, back into the Red Zone. He wanted to scream. He wanted to demand answers from his uncle. Myriad questions raced through his mind . . . but they all disappeared as soon as he saw the look on Lot's face.

Her eyes were wide as saucers as she met his gaze. "Sorry, Dev," she whimpered. "There was nothing we could do."

Eema's huge security husk loomed over them. Her yellow emoji face glowered as she kept her guns trained on Lot and Mason. They whined to life, rising in a pitch that Dev knew would end in a devastating blast.

"Eema! Stand down!"

Eema's guns suddenly lowered as the machine relaxed. They spun around to see Lee striding through the doorway, his team following, weapons raised. Charles Parker followed, his cuffs drawn so tightly together, he couldn't move his arms.

Dev felt helpless. His few minutes of horrified hesitation in the cabin had meant defeat.

"Impressive, Dev." Lee grinned and pointed to his troops fanning out around them. "These guys are the most highly skilled mercenaries in the world. The best money can buy, and yet you constantly kept ahead of them." He looked behind him at Charles Parker. "Quite a feat, don't you think, Prof? A real testament to all your hard work here."

Charles Parker remained silent. He was looking at the open door of the cabin.

"I've been inside," said Dev, his voice cracking with the strain. "I know what you do here."

Lee's confusion was not lost on Dev. He also saw the shock on Lot's and Mason's faces. Charles Parker refused to meet his nephew's gaze.

"But I guess I don't *need to know*." Dev fought to keep his tears back. "I was grown in one of those tubes, wasn't

I? Just one of the many Inventory projects the World Consortium dabbled with, then discarded when things didn't work out to their advantage."

Charles Parker cleared his throat, and for the first time Dev could ever remember, he heard a tinge of regret in his uncle's voice. "These tanks come from a project originally created in North Korea. They were an attempt to create a super-soldier – the most elite warrior on the battlefield. Of course it didn't quite work, although the technology was years beyond anything the rest of the world had. So the World Consortium did what it does. It sent out a task force to steal the technology to bring it back here where nobody could dabble with it."

"Except you?"

Charles Parker finally met his gaze. The regret in his voice had vanished completely, replaced by the familiar jaded tone his uncle always wore when dealing with Dev.

"We needed something more advanced than Eema to guard this place. A security system that couldn't be hacked and could think for itself."

Charles's eyes bored into Dev, who was rapidly trying to sift through the overwhelming evidence he had uncovered.

Lee clapped his hands, breaking the moment. "OK,

what a lovely dysfunctional family reunion. We've all got problems, kid. And yours are about to get worse if you don't start cooperating." He gestured around the room. "Iron Fist. Go fetch. Or I will let Eema here start making holes in your friends."

WELL-PLANNED IMPROVISATION

"Psst!"

Volta turned around at the noise, glad to have a distraction from the tense scene unfolding in front of him. He saw the boy's lips move but heard only a low mumbling. He shuffled closer. "Speak up, boy."

Mason tilted his head towards Kwolek and raised his voice a little. He had mumbled deliberately to lure the man closer. "What happened to your girlfriend's arm?"

Volta followed his gaze towards Kwolek and sighed. *Girlfriend* was clearly something he wished for. "It's a long story, but quite incredible," he whispered back.

"I'd love to know, but. . ." said Mason.

It took just seconds for Volta to understand. Lot dropped to her knees behind the mercenary the exact instant that Mason shouldered all his bulk into him. It was an old trick, but neither Lot nor Mason could have taken the big man down on their own.

Volta's arms windmilled as he tried to catch his balance, but it was no use. Mason watched as, almost in slow motion, Volta stumbled with a shout.

The group spun round just in time to see him drop his rifle and then lurch in the other direction to avoid it firing the moment it hit the floor.

But he wasn't looking where he was going. Mason winced as Volta stumbled straight into the nearest energy shield.

There was an enormous bang and then a haze of smoke where Volta had been.

"GO!" Lot yelled as she jumped to her feet, pulling Mason after her. "Dev – go for it!"

The confusion over Volta's sudden disappearance was enough for Lot and Mason to put a gap between them and their pursuers before the mercenaries opened fire.

Lot sidestepped as the floor in front of her exploded. She rolled behind the cover of a bulldozer-sized exhibit, unslung the AirCannon from her back and aimed at the twins, who were running towards her. She pulled the trigger.

The blast of ultra-compressed air smacked full force into the twins. They were flung backwards – somersaulting over and over before smashing into the wall.

Mason high-fived Lot. "That was *awesome*."

Dev watched in mute shock as Volta was vaporized. He couldn't move – until Lot's voice pierced his brain.

"Dev – go for it!"

The words broke him from his stupor and he sprinted towards the Iron Fist exhibit. He hadn't formed a conscious plan, but his muscles appeared to be working on instinct alone.

"Dev!" Lot shouted as she and Mason caught up with him. "Don't touch it! You saw what happened to that guy."

But Dev had fixed his goal firmly fixed in his mind: get Iron Fist and get out of the Inventory as swiftly as possible. He was so focused on the Iron Fist that he only saw Kwolek at the last moment

But before Kwolek could reach out to grab Dev, the massive rolling form of Eema struck the bionic mercenary from the side like a bowling ball. The robot rapidly unfolded, four legs securing her in place – two gun arms whirling in position. Her emoji face had turned from yellow to red.

Eema was back – fully downloaded in her battle husk, and straining for a fight.

Kwolek was on her feet in time to bat one of Eema's arms aside. The energy blast hit the ceiling, destroying several lights and causing a section of supporting girders to collapse.

Before Eema could fire again, Kwolek unleashed a series of savage punches, her bionic exoskeleton repeatedly denting the husk's advanced armour.

Dev was stunned by Kwolek's speed as she ducked another energy blast and sidestepped a vicious punch from a pair of smaller service arms that had unfolded from the recesses of the husk.

Every punch Kwolek landed on Eema kicked up a fury of sparks. The emoji face registered each hit by glowing redder and redder. Although Dev knew the AI robot was incapable of feeling pain, he still felt sorry for her.

Eema tried to swing at Kwolek with a gun arm, but this time her opponent grabbed hold and vaulted gracefully *on to* the arm. Kwolek delivered a series of bionic punches at the robot's shoulder, intending to snap the gun away from the body.

With each blow, Eema reeled. Dev realized that if he didn't do something, then Kwolek was going to win this fight.

With a bellow, Dev rushed for Kwolek, whose back was to him as she rained blows on Eema. He knew there was no way he could leap up on to Eema, but still he knew he had to do something.

But he was wrong. Just like when he had first punched Mason, Dev's body surprised him by performing a feat of strength way beyond what he could normally achieve. He soared through the air and landed on the gun arm, just behind Kwolek.

The mercenary turned and threw a mechanically assisted punch over her shoulder, the impact of which would cleave his skull in two. Dev didn't duck. He didn't see the fist until it was centimetres away from his face. He focused instead on her exoskeleton, staring at the pulses of colour that criss-crossed the metal; colours that only he could see. Discordant chimes filled his ears, which changed to mellow musical tones as he reached his fingers towards a single hidden circuit. His fingernails dug in and he felt something pop.

"What have you done?" Kwolek screeched. She was frozen in position, her fist hanging in the air a millimetre from Dev's nose. No matter how much strain registered on Kwolek's face, she couldn't move.

"Looks like you froze," grinned Dev. He had found the crucial control on her shoulder. His unique synaesthesia had guided him to this one chip that would cause a short circuit the moment he pulled it free. Kwolek was frozen in place, a prisoner in her own bionic exoskeleton.

Dev leapt to the ground as Eema threw Kwolek across the room. She landed hard on the floor, without shifting position.

Dev ran a hand across Eema's dented armour. The robot's furious red face turned back to a familiar smiling yellow one.

"I thought they had partitioned you in the network," smiled Dev.

"Once your uncle entered this room, the automated security system opened up. It's separate from the rest of the Inventory so I was able to download into this husk."

"It's good to have you—" Dev began, but Eema

suddenly moved and arced around him – absorbing the sonic blasts from Fermi and another soldier, who were both charging forward.

Lot had seen them make their move too. She fired the AirCannon, but her aim was off and instead she struck Lee, who was scrambling towards a fallen rifle. Lee howled in pain and tumbled back against a wall.

Eema whirled the gun on the remaining mercenaries. Instead of a deadly energy blast, a yellow gloop shot out and struck them in mid-run, instantly covering them. The slime crystallized over them, bonding them to the floor, able to breathe but not move.

"OK, you go and get my uncle," Dev instructed Eema. "I'm getting the Iron Fist."

Eema swivelled around. "It's too late for your uncle."

Dev looked across the warehouse to see Lee pointing a shaking pistol at Charles Parker.

"It's time for you to leave," said Eema urgently. One of her arms indicated the domed cage at the far end of the chamber. "Use the teleporter."

"What about my uncle?"

"I will look after him. You're more important, Dev."

Eema almost sounded as if she was pleading. "OK, but not without the Iron Fist." Dev turned back to the shimmering energy shield and concentrated. As he focused on the chaotic fizz of dots, they slowly resolved into a solid shape: a gauntlet, constructed from tiny metallic-blue plates, as he had seen in the Inventory's archive picture. Small spheres poked from the surface, which Dev recognized as miniature Tesla coils. It was old, a relic; not the impressive gadget he had been expecting.

Lot's warning almost broke his concentration. "Dev!"

Dev's eyes hurt as he kept the Iron Fist in focus. He slowly reached for it.

"Dev! Don't!" screamed Lot.

But it was too late – Dev's hands sunk into the energy shield that had annihilated Volta. . .

THE ESCAPE

Dev felt a fizz of electricity as the hairs on his arm stood on end, but there was no lethal energy pulse to tear him apart. Although he had never seen energy shields like this before, Dev instinctively knew what to do. He knew it was nothing more than a potentially deadly optical illusion.

Dev had never been a good listener, especially when his uncle had delivered his sermons on quantum physics. Nevertheless, he recalled Charles Parker talking about particles able to be in two places at once, only settling on a place – or state – once they had been observed. It was called the "observer effect". He had asked his physics teacher about it, but had been met with a perplexed look and told to go home before he was placed on detention.

Once Dev had focused on the Iron Fist it snapped into view like an optical illusion, and the swarming particles vanished because they had formed into the solid invention now sitting on the plinth. By simply switching his perception, Dev could force the particles to switch between the object and the shield. All anybody else could see was the energy vortex. They were not observing it correctly. Only Dev could see the truth. He wondered if that was part of his artificially created abilities.

But the moment he picked up the Iron Fist he heard a collective gasp from around him. Clearly, to everybody else's eyes, the shield had vanished and the gadget had instantly appeared.

"Dev! Don't try to leave." Lee shoved the pistol against Charles Parker's head.

Dev looked between the thief and his uncle. Charles Parker was watching curiously, with a hint of a smile tugging the corner of his lips.

"You've lost," Dev snarled defiantly at Lee. "Eema – cover us!"

The Iron Fist was heavy. Dev had expected it to be light, like most modern carbon-fibre gadgets. He was forced to hold it with both hands as he sprinted towards the teleporter at the top of the tiered steps. Lot and Mason kept close, with Eema rolling just behind them. Lee fired several shots, but they pinged harmlessly from Eema's armour.

Ahead, a dozen steps led to the raised platform that overlooked the warehouse. The teleporter was a circular platform surrounded by curved metal poles that formed a spherical cage with gaps easily wide enough for Lot and Mason to enter.

Dev heard his uncle shout a warning. He couldn't make out the words – but Charles Parker was silenced as Lee cracked him over the head. Dev watched his uncle crumple unconscious to the floor.

Dev hesitated between returning for his uncle and fleeing. He knew the Iron Fist was too dangerous to fall into the enemy's hands. He forced himself to think of the greater good. "Eema, come with us!"

"My place is to protect the Inventory and you. If you go, I will still have achieved a significant portion of my protocols."

Dev wanted to argue, but Mason pulled him into the

cage. "You heard the robot. It wants to stay. We want to leave."

"Activating teleportation procedure," said Eema.

Before Dev could protest, the bars around them began to spin, each overlapping the next with increasing fury. They moved so fast, it became impossible to distinguish between the individual bars, and Dev felt as if they were becoming encased in a solid metal shell.

Their ears popped – then the bars slowed down before jerking to a halt.

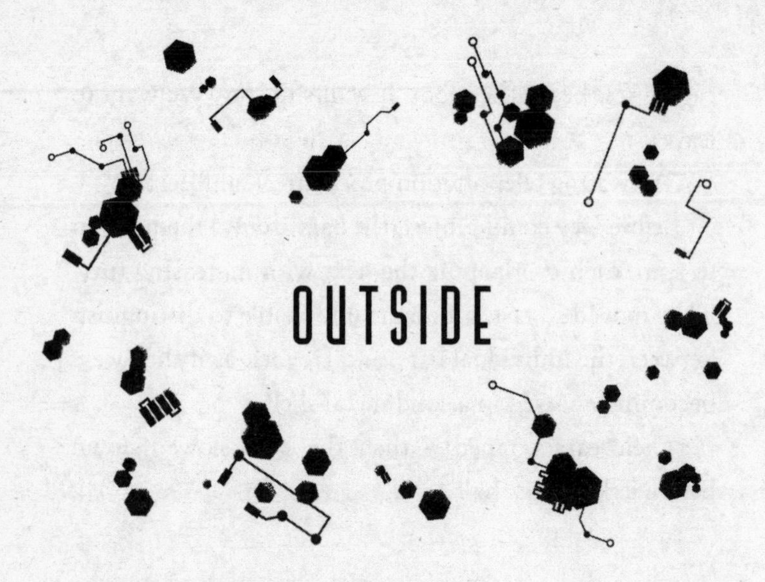

OUTSIDE

Dev blinked as his eyes adjusted to the darkness around them. It took him a moment to recognize his surroundings. They were in one of the barns. The cold winter's air smelled like a bonfire.

"Did we make it out?" asked Lot, looking around.

Dev walked cautiously towards the door and stopped as a spotlight suddenly illuminated, picking him out. Carefully he raised his arm to shield his eyes, not wanting to drop the Iron Fist in the snow.

"Devon?"

Instantly he recognized the woman's voice from the ELF transmission. His eyes quickly grew accustomed to the light and he saw Sergeant Wade. She was looking at him as if she were seeing a ghost. He became aware of dozens of World Consortium soldiers behind her and beyond them, the smouldering remains of what had once been his home. The farmhouse was missing an entire wing, which was now a tangle of scorched bricks.

Dev felt Lot's hand on his shoulder. "Dev, your house . . . you've lost everything."

Dev stared at Sergeant Wade, who was quick to compose herself. "Dev . . . you have the Iron Fist. Well done! We'll take that from here." Then, almost as an afterthought, she added, "Are you all OK? Not hurt?" She reached for the Iron Fist, but Dev moved back protectively.

"I don't think so. We risked our lives and the intruders are still trapped below, with my uncle."

"Well done," repeated Wade with a big smile.

"Which makes me wonder why it was so important to get this out." Dev lifted the Iron Fist a little.

Sergeant Wade's smile stayed in place, but the rest of her face betrayed a sudden nervousness. "In the wrong hands it could be used for terrible things. That's why you must hand it over for safety."

Dev didn't move. Mason and Lot shuffled closer to

him, feeling stronger as a unit. They had detected the subtle shift in the surrounding soldiers' body language. They were tense, as if waiting for an order to spring into action.

"And *you're* the right hands?" said Dev. He kept his gaze on the woman and saw a twitch at the corner of her mouth. A smile? Or had he touched a nerve?

"We are the World Consortium, of course we're the right hands!" Wade looked at her soldiers, then waved at them to back away. "You're alarming these poor children. Give them some room; they've been through hell down there."

Dev's thoughts flicked back to the cloning chamber. He was unsure who he could believe.

"There's one thing that puzzles me," said Dev in a low voice. He twisted the Iron Fist around to get a proper look at it. "This was already held safely down there. How would the Collector know how to use it? It's not as if *anybody* can use what's in the Inventory."

Wade shifted from foot to foot and rubbed her chin in an attempt to mask her discomfort. "The Collector . . . that's a name he gave himself. He doesn't have a name. All he has is a number. . ."

That struck a chord with Dev. "A number?"

"He was called Seven."

The dominoes in Dev's mind cascaded into a full picture. "That's because he was a clone." Wade's silence confirmed this. "He was manufactured down there. Just like me."

Wade couldn't hide her surprise. "Devon . . . look, there are things you need to know – but nobody had wanted you to find out like this. You don't remember your mother, do you?"

Dev was speaking as if the words were being pulled out of him. "It's you, isn't it?"

"Wow," said Lot. "This is like one of those bad daytime-TV shows."

Wade burst into puzzled laughter. "What? No. Of course I'm not. Do I look that old?" She pressed on before Dev could answer. "It's important that you know—"

A blue flash burned Dev's retina. His ears thumped as the air pressure changed and the noise around him fell into thick silence. He felt himself sway as a wave of dizziness rattled through his head. The effect was over in seconds.

Wade stood before him, perfectly motionless, like a movie on pause. Even the snowflakes were suspended in the air around her. Dev drew in a breath as he looked around. The Consortium soldiers were motionless. A Chinook was frozen in mid-air, rotors rigidly in place as it defied gravity. Lot was by his side like a waxwork. He pressed a finger against her cheek – it felt like solid marble.

"A stasis bomb," said a voice from behind.

Dev slowly turned. He knew what to expect, but seeing the towering figure of the Collector in the flesh was somehow creepier than anything his imagination had been able to muster up.

The Collector adjusted his yellow-lensed glasses with one hand, and gestured around with the other. "They'll be held in place, unaware of our little discussion."

Even though Dev couldn't see the villain's eyes, he sensed they were locked on the Iron Fist. He found his voice. "So you're a clone like me?"

"You were created as my replacement, just as the others you saw down there will replace you." The Collector looked him up and down. "I see they have improved some aspects. Your synaesthesia, those heightened surges allowing you to run faster and leap higher in times of crisis ... they were all designed in a lab. Manipulated by the very cloning technology the Inventory was created to stop people using in the first place. Designed, as I was, by good old Uncle Parker."

Dev felt sick, weak at the knees. He stumbled against Lot for support, but she didn't budge.

The Collector continued with mocking tones. "When I escaped from this prison, the Consortium saw me as a threat, so they changed the Inventory's entire security procedures – ensuring that I could no longer enter and objects couldn't leave."

"But they can leave." Dev held the Iron Fist aloft.

"Only when taken out by the right key. A very special key."

Dev blinked in confusion. "I don't have a key. It's just me and..." He trailed off as he read between the lines. A chill ran down his spin as the Collector lowered his voice.

"Dev. *You* are the key."

FIFTY SHADES OF DUMB

"Impossible. . ." Dev spluttered.

The Collector slowly paced around him. "You are the Inventory's greatest treasure. A living biological key able to bring any item out, designed with abilities tailored perfectly to fix, repair and keep everything within the Inventory running. All those years you smuggled out small items to play with on the farm . . . that was just your uncle testing the effectiveness of the system. *You* are the last line of security. *You are the Iron Fist.*"

Dev's mind reeled. The idea that he was a living key . . . it was something he couldn't process. He looked blankly at the relic in his hand.

"Considering you needed me alive, your mercenaries went out of their way to kill me."

"Trust me, Dev, they are not really such bad shots. You needed some simple motivation. Survival."

Dev scowled, feeling a growing sense of hatred towards the Collector. "So that makes me a superior version of you."

The Collector removed his yellow glasses, and Dev couldn't contain a gasp of shock. The criminal's eyes were white. Where other people had an iris and pupil, the fiend had nothing but a smooth milky-white eyeball. Dev turned away, repulsed.

"I can see you perfectly," said the Collector, tugging at the corner of his eye with one finger, revealing more sickening white. "My eyes never developed the way they should, yet I can see across a wider range of spectrums. I can see the ultraviolet waves pumping from the environment sensor in the grass. I can see the heat from your cheeks when you lie. I bear witness to the radiation pulses of supernova burning the night sky!" He extended his arms as if embracing the heavens.

Dev took an involuntary step backwards. "I'm sorry you've got freaky eyes, but that's not my fault. I thought we were running from a deadly clever enemy, when all along you were nothing more than a bunch of ordinary thieves, looking to steal this." He indicated the gauntlet.

"*Ordinary* thieves? Ha! We are *exceptional* thieves! You still don't grasp the scope of what I have achieved."

"I take issue with the word 'thief'," said Lee, emerging from the barn and buttoning his jacket against the cold. He looked pale from his teleportation trip. "I'm a skilled technician." He gave a respectful nod towards the Collector. "I gotta hand it to you, I never thought we'd get past the last line of security. That was a stroke of genius getting him to flee with this thing, believing it was of real value."

Dev looked at the Iron Fist in his arms. "I don't get it . . . if you claim I'm Iron Fist . . . then this?"

Lee scoffed loudly. "Ain't you fifty shades of dumb? I switched the Inventory files when I gained access to the system just in case you got online. That way you would believe that this –" he waved at the gauntlet "– was the precious artefact. Really, you think a piece of junk salvaged from a bunch of scrap was what we wanted?"

The Collector pulled a journal from his pocket, the same one Pavel had retrieved from the Moscow apartment. He wagged it in front of Dev. "It's all logged in here. The private journal of Professor Yenin – the man hired by the World Consortium to dream up the impregnable security system. It was within these pages I discovered that you were the living key, Dev."

Dev was silent as he processed the information. His whole world, his entire reason for being, was far different from anything he had imagined. "So Eema was never designed to guard the *Inventory* – she was only designed to guard *me*?"

All the while Dev had felt bitter about living under Eema's dictatorial eye when all along she had been there to protect him. And he in turn had been created to protect the Inventory, the very place he longed to be free of.

"But now I'm outside..." Dev stopped in his tracks. He was the *key*. By leaving the Inventory he had unlocked the door and left it open for the Collector and his team.

Dev suddenly felt very stupid. He had played into their hands from the very beginning. He sighed so deeply that his body shook, his shoulders sagging in defeat.

"You win. Here, you might as well have this piece of junk back."

He lifted the gauntlet with one hand, his other

slipping inside to bear the weight. It was an innocent motion that didn't arouse anybody's suspicions – just as Dev had intended.

The moment his hand slipped into the gauntlet, he felt as if he had immersed it in warm water. His synaesthesia kicked into action and suddenly he knew what the gauntlet was. He could sense its potential.

He knew exactly how to activate it.

There was a gentle pressure along his forearm, and the tiny Tesla coils flared to life, powered by the tiny current running naturally through his body. Dev couldn't help but smile when he saw the look of horror creeping over Lee's face as the metallic plates along the relic rapidly expanded out across his arm with a clicking noise, reminiscent of a camera snapping photos.

"Oops," he said. "I think I have just activated it. Why don't we see what this piece of rubbish is really capable of?"

IRON FIST

The transformation was so fluid that it was difficult to follow what was happening. Dev glimpsed tiny hexagonal plates, no bigger than his thumbnail, spread up his arm and across his body. Within seconds he felt them slide up his throat like a layer of mud, then tickle his face before covering his eyes, plunging him into blackness.

The claustrophobia would have panicked most people, but Dev kept his wits. He reasoned that an artefact of this importance wouldn't try to kill him. The darkness tuned his other senses. He was still able to breathe through the metallic plates and, as they spread, the gauntlet's weight on his arm decreased until it was perfectly distributed across his body and felt no heavier than a thick winter coat.

His sixth-sense synaesthesia was chiming too. Pleasant pastel colours swirled before his eyes, assuring him all was right and the machine was operating exactly as an advanced suit of mechanized battle armour should. No wonder Wade had been nervous about him activating it. It was a lot more than a piece of salvaged junk.

Then light appeared – real light, not the swirling colour of his synaesthesia – and he could suddenly see the farm.

His first observation, looking at the objects around him, was that he appeared taller, as if standing on a rooftop.

He imagined just how cool he must be looking right now.

Lee and the Collector reeled backwards as the gauntlet enveloped Dev's arm and spread across his body in a series of small metal plates.

"Wow," said Lee, rooted to the spot.

Following the rough contours of Dev's body, the

mech swelled in size until it was the height of the barn, yet inside he couldn't judge if he remained the same size or had grown with it. Mechanical muscles flexed. He twisted his hand and twigged his fingers – the suit mirroring his actions perfectly. This was a suit built for one purpose: war.

The Collector warily retreated. He hadn't been expecting *this*. His fingers accessed the control panel built into his glove and the stasis bomb folded with a loud pop. The figures who had been held in its grip were suddenly galvanized into motion.

Sergeant Wade looked around in confusion. Dev had gone and a giant mech had appeared in his place.

Gunfire erupted from the soldiers, equally confused. Bullets pinged from the metal giant, and Dev could feel the impact of each as if he had been punched. The impacts jolted him into action and he spun around, arm raised. The movements were smooth, as if he wasn't wearing a giant suit.

Dev screamed for them to stop shooting, but the suit didn't amplify his voice; rather, it came out muffled and drowned in the automatic gunfire. He realized he was as much a target as the Collector.

The Collector himself had dashed towards the

barn for cover. Gunfire rained down on Dev's arm and thigh. In desperation, he reached for the Chinook as it took off. The mech's super-sized arms were easily able to pluck it from the air. The terrified pilot tried to accelerate his ascent – and Dev felt his feet skid on the ice. He quickly caught his balance and, with a grunt of effort, swung the helicopter around to block the hail of bullets.

The Consortium soldiers ceased fire as soon as their first bullets clipped the Chinook. Dev gave a karate chop – and the mech suit followed his actions. With a tortured squeal of metal, the mech's hands severed the forward set of rotors.

Dev rolled the stricken Chinook across the ground, the second set of rotors tearing apart as they struck the frozen ground. The fuselage tumbled towards the Consortium troops – forcing them to flee out of its path.

That was the distraction Dev needed to focus his attention on the Collector. He ran after the villain, who was following Lee towards one of the few barns left standing. The Collector held Lot by the collar. Lee dragged Mason, his pistol aimed at the boy's ribs.

The Collector stopped as the mech loomed over them. Dev could sense the mech's controls; he knew the machine's secret. With a simple motion he activated the weapons. A pair of rocket launchers unfolded from the mech's shoulders, recessed guns elevating from the wrists. He had no time to marvel at the incredible miniaturization process that had packed everything into a single gauntlet. He had his friends to save.

"This needs to end," said the Collector. "Deactivate or. . ." He let the threat hang in the air.

Dev considered unleashing the mighty firepower at his disposal. It would probably turn the Collector into a smoking crater. It would almost definitely kill Lot too.

"I never bluff, Devon," said the Collector. He indicated to his glove. "This is called a dimensionalizer. Watch."

A stream of nanoparticles rose from his glove and circled Lot's head. Dev had no idea what the threat was, but the swarm couldn't be good news. He glanced around and noticed Wade had regrouped her soldiers, who silently formed a semicircle behind the mech. At least she now knew Dev was inside the machine.

With a flick of his wrist, the Collector guided his swarm to the nearest soldier. The cloud whipped out so fast the man didn't see it coming. He was suddenly flattened into a two-dimensional image. His colleagues around him quickly backed away as the man shattered into countless particles.

The Collector placed his gloved hand at the back of Lot's neck. "Her life is in your hands."

Lot refused to whimper or cry, but even she couldn't stop her lip trembling with fright.

Dev snarled, but he had no choice. With a surge of clicking plates, he deactivated the mech. It folded rapidly away into the heavy gauntlet – leaving Dev standing before the Collector, his hand half out of the device.

"OK," said Dev. "Here's what will happen. Release Lot and Mason. Put them in the barn. Once they're safe, you can have this . . . and me."

"NO!" screamed Lot. "Don't do it, Dev!"

The Collector tightened his grip on her collar, choking her to silence. "A fair exchange. Lee." He nodded towards the barn.

Lee was wary. "You sure about this?"

The Collector's gaze never left Dev. "He may be many things, but a liar . . . no. You're a man of your word, aren't you, Devon? Just like me."

Dev felt sick to stomach. He didn't want to be reminded that he and this fiend were the same. Is *this* what he would grow up to be?

"Dev, don't. . ." pleaded Lot.

"It's the only way, Lot. Remember what your dad told you: *keep flying high*."

He saw the puzzled expression on Lot's face before the Collector shoved her into the barn and Lee dragged the door closed.

The Collector extended his hand. "As you can see, I am a man of my word."

Dev regarded the gauntlet. "This is a powerful weapon. I got a sense that it can do *so* much more."

"Indeed. Lee was mistaken that it was mere scrap. The gauntlet is an omega-class device. Otherwise it wouldn't have been stored in the Red Zone."

"So I have unlocked the Inventory for you," said Dev. "What are you going to do with it?"

The Collector made an odd hawking sound, the closest he had come to a laugh. "Devon, your thinking is so *one*-dimensional. I have *already* done what I needed." He indicated to the battlefield around them. "Smoke and mirrors, Dev. While you and the Consortium have been wasting time up here, my task force below has been looting the collection."

Yet again Dev felt as if the rug had been pulled from under his feet. "You used me as a decoy."

The Collector tilted his head. "Clones. Your design flaw is your predictability."

Dev opened his mouth to speak, but at that moment the side of the barn exploded in a rain of rotting wood as an aircraft burst out and hovered behind Lee and the Collector.

The vehicle was no bigger than a family car; wires and piping hung from its belly, and a pair of hemispheres bolted to the side to provide an electromagnetic lift. It was the very machine Dev had stopped Lot from uncovering when they'd found Mason in the barn – a next-generation HoverCar.

The craft purred as it hovered. Through the bubble canopy, Dev could see Lot and Mason seated inside. Lot was at the controls. She had understood the hidden meaning in his words – *keep flying high,* her father's motto. Now she was gracefully demonstrating the skills she had learned with him – well, almost. The aircraft wobbled as she fought the cyclic control stick and simultaneously balanced the collective lever to keep them steady in the air. Mason controlled a joystick that moved a cannon bolted on to the aircraft's nose.

"You need to learn when to give up!" snapped Lee

as he shot at the aircraft, bullets ricocheting from the reinforced canopy. "You're becoming tedious."

Mason returned fire. A pulse of energy somersaulted Lee against a pile of wreckage.

The Collector fired his dimensionalizer.

Lot managed to jink the aircraft to the side as the cloud of nanoparticles shot past and smothered the remains of the barn. With an ear-piercing crack, the entire structure snapped from three dimensions to two – before toppling down and shattering into countless pieces.

The Collector turned to flee – but ran straight into a giant fist.

Literally.

Dev had used the distraction to activate the mech suit. The massive fist struck the Collector, knocking him out.

He spun to follow Lee, who had sprinted off the moment the barn had shattered. Dev was just in time to see Lee unfold what looked like a rubber disc and toss it on the floor. Dev recognized it as a portable hole.

Lee flicked a casual salute – and jumped into the hole. The hole sucked in on itself and vanished with a loud pop.

At Sergeant Wade's signal, the Consortium troops sprang into action. They cuffed the Collector, taking care to remove his dimensionalizer glove. Even unconscious, the Collector was a lethal weapon.

Dev deactivated the mech and watched Lot make a bumpy landing, although his mind was reeling with the cascade of revelations and the fact they had stopped the Collector.

Mason and Lot climbed out of the craft and ran to Dev, who was surprised when Lot tightly hugged him.

"You OK?" she asked, finally letting go. Dev nodded.

Mason watched the Collector being dragged off. "Where did Lee go?"

"He scored a hole in one," muttered Dev. He could see Mason didn't get it, but couldn't summon the energy to explain. The sight of his smouldering home depressed him just as much as the wicked truths he had uncovered.

Sergeant Wade patted him on the shoulder. "Dev, you have done some amazing things here. You should feel proud."

Dev shook his head. Pride was the last emotion he was feeling. "I need to go back and find my uncle."

"Your uncle will be OK."

"I hope so. Some of the thieves are still down there.

We need to get them before they have a chance to escape."

The numbing truth was dawning on Dev. After seeing how easily Lee had slipped away, he wondered if there really was anybody left down there. Since the Collector had lured him out to deactivate the Iron First security, they could come and go as they pleased.

The Collector had said it himself: *they were exceptional thieves.*

OUT OF STOCK

Charles Parker looked shell-shocked as he gazed at the empty shelves in the Yellow Zone. From the moment Dev and his friends had escaped the Red Zone, Charles had felt a blow to his head and lost consciousness – only to awake to see Dev and Sergeant Wade kneeling over him with concern. His head had been bandaged, but he'd refused to be airlifted to a Consortium base for further medical attention. His first priority was the Inventory.

Dev had noticed his first priority wasn't his nephew. While that would have hurt him in the past, now he accepted the bitter pill that he was essentially just another item in the Inventory. He was an artificial clone. Did that mean he wasn't really a person? Dev didn't want to think about the consequences of that.

Sergeant Wade had greeted Charles Parker as an old friend, but as soon as the extent of the theft became apparent, they both lapsed into shocked silence.

A few items remained, but the majority of the exhibits – some the size of aircraft carriers – had simply vanished, and the surviving thieves with them. The sight of row after row of empty spaces made Dev feel sick. The Collector had toyed with him by trying to barter for the gauntlet, when he was in fact stalling for time while the surviving members of his team below cleaned out the inventions they really coveted.

The real Eema was discovered in a partitioned section of the network. Lee had cleverly replaced her with a simple AI system that acted like Eema and insisted that Dev leave the complex.

Dev found no satisfaction when the real Eema stated that her priority would have been to stop Dev leaving via the teleporter . . . *at any cost.*

Charles Parker confirmed that the moment Dev had been through the teleporter, the security surrounding the objects in the Inventory had been deactivated.

Dev was indeed the key to that. Without the security offered by him, the objects could now be moved out or destroyed. It was the Achilles heel in the security, the one that had been only uncovered in the journal the Collector had obtained. Some boffin in the World Consortium had pointed out that, in times of crisis, Inventory stock might have to be removed so it could be used. No matter how good security was, once it was deactivated, it was useless.

How so many objects were moved in such a short space of time, nobody knew, but Charles suspected they had employed the range of teleporting devices that had once filled an entire shelf. With those they could have easily inserted a whole platoon of men to help take the gadgets. Dev pointed out a stasis bomb could have been used on them all, and they would never have known. The truth was there were many ways to plunder the unsecure Inventory.

The pressing matter now was to trace where they had been taken. Charles was confident the team of Consortium forensic scientists would find out. But for now there was little to do other than mop up the mess.

Dev dropped the gauntlet back on to its plinth in the Red Zone and sighed. "I feel so stupid."

Lot patted him on the arm. She didn't know what to say. Mason looked away. He had been feeling guilty for the part he had played in letting the thieves in. He was so repentant that he kept apologizing to everybody he spoke to.

Charles Parker placed his hand on Dev's shoulder. It was supposed to be a comforting gesture, but coming from Dev's uncle it just felt weird. "There's no way you could have known."

There were still many questions burning in Dev's brain. "So all of this was conducted for Shadow Helix? What is it?" His uncle hesitated. "And I'd better warn you," Dev added, "if I ever hear the phrase *you don't need to know,* then things are going to get violent."

"The truth is we don't know. For many years Shadow Helix has been off the radar. Oh, we know it's around, orchestrating things from afar, but we only see their lackeys – like the Collector."

Dev sighed. "So all those lethal gadgets are now loose out there. What's going to happen to them?"

Charles Parker was silent.

"What's going to happen?"

Charles cleared his throat. "*You've* got to get them back."

"Me?" said Dev. "I thought that was the Consortium's job?"

"Devon, you were ... created for a specific reason." Charles Parker ignored the pained look on Dev's face. "You can control and speak to each and every one of those devices. We need you out there." He pointed upwards. "In the real world, where you can hunt them down and bring them back."

Dev couldn't find the words to answer.

Charles's voice softened. "Devon ... Dev ... don't be fooled. Whether you were created in a tube or any other way, it doesn't make you less of a human. You'll always be my nephew."

The thaw in his uncle's cold demeanour took Dev by surprise. It reminded him of better days when his uncle hadn't seemed so distant and lost in his work.

Charles continued. "After all, that's what you were made for."

The warmth Dev had been feeling vanished instantly. Dev shucked his uncle's hand away and turned to Mason and Lot. Lot gave a smile, that infectious one he'd always admired. "We'll help you," she said.

"Like it or not, as of now, you are both working for the World Consortium," said Charles Parker.

"Yes, sir!" snapped Mason, throwing his best salute and beaming with pride.

Between Mason, Lot and his uncle, Dev couldn't help but think what an unlikely team they made. Mason had proved, against all odds, not to be a complete idiot and waste of space. Dev was forced to admit that he had guts. Plus, it wasn't all so bad. At least he would get to spend a little more time with Lot. . .

"I accept the mission," said Dev, forcing a smile.

"Good." Charles Parker nodded and began walking away. He didn't see his nephew's expression harden. Dev had many more questions for his "uncle".

And he was pretty sure he wouldn't like the answers. . .

Andy Briggs is a screenwriter,
graphic novelist, author
and conservationist.
Follow him online:
andybriggs.co.uk
@abriggswriter